William Peterfield Trent

John Milton

A short Study of his Life and Works

William Peterfield Trent

John Milton
A short Study of his Life and Works

ISBN/EAN: 9783337055318

Printed in Europe, USA, Canada, Australia, Japan

Cover: Foto ©Raphael Reischuk / pixelio.de

More available books at **www.hansebooks.com**

JOHN MILTON

A SHORT STUDY OF HIS LIFE AND WORKS

The
Co

JOHN MILTON

A SHORT STUDY OF HIS LIFE AND WORKS

BY

WILLIAM P. TRENT

AUTHOR OF "WILLIAM GILMORE SIMMS," "SOUTHERN STATESMEN OF THE OLD RÉGIME," "ROBERT E. LEE," ETC.

New York
THE MACMILLAN COMPANY
LONDON: MACMILLAN & CO., LTD.
1899

Norwood Press
J. S. Cushing & Co. — Berwick & Smith
Norwood Mass. U.S.A.

TO

RICHARD GARNETT, LL.D.

Of the British Museum

WHO TO HIS WELL-DESERVED FAME AS POET, SCHOLAR

AND CRITIC

AND TO HIS POWER AND CHARM AS A FULL MAN

ADDS THE DISTINCTION OF BEING

A LOVER AND JUDICIOUS BIOGRAPHER OF MILTON

This Little Volume is Inscribed

IN FRIENDSHIP AND GRATITUDE

PREFACE

This book is a result of a conviction forced upon me by an experience of many years as a teacher of literature, that we Anglo-Saxons do not honor Milton as we should do, that we too frequently misunderstand him and neglect him. He is rapidly passing — if, indeed, he has not already passed — into the class of authors whom we talk about oftener than we read. In view of this fact I have here ventured to tell over again the story of his life and achievements in the hope that I may win him more lovers and readers.

It may, of course, be deemed a presumptuous undertaking, for there is nothing new to say after Professor Masson's herculean labors, of which I have taken full advantage, and Mark Pattison and Dr. Garnett have covered the field admirably in their smaller volumes. But I have thought that the new book always has an advantage as a literary missioner, if I may use the phrase, through the very fact of its novelty, and I have also hoped that a somewhat unusual grouping and proportioning of the most important biographical and critical materials might arrest the attention of at least a few of the many souls to whom Milton has become a name and nothing more. But perhaps I have trusted rather to the naturally contagious effects of an enthusiastic treatment of a poet who has inspired me with reverence since my earliest years. If this hope fail me, I shall at least not repent of having paid a vain tribute to his memory, for popular neglect can never really dim the lustre of Milton's fame, nor can an injudicious panegyric hurt it, and it is always a spiritual advantage to a man to give utterance to a love and enthusiasm for a sublime character that have grown with his growth and strengthened with his strength.

W. P. TRENT.

SEWANEE, TENN.,
January 9, 1899.

Hearty thanks are hereby given to Messrs. Longmans, Green, and Company for their kind permission to use in Chapters III., IV., and V. of Part II. considerable matter first employed in my edition of "L'Allegro" and other poems in their "English Classics," edited by my friend, Professor George R. Carpenter, whose consent has also been granted. Much of the matter in Chapters VIII. and IX. of Part II. will be found in the *Protestant Episcopal Review* for April and May, 1899; while the first part is expanded from an article published in the *Sewanee Review* for January, 1897.

CONTENTS

PART I. — LIFE

CHAPTER I

CHAPTER II

CHAPTER III

PART II. — WORKS

CHAPTER I

CHAPTER II

CHAPTER III

CHAPTER IV

CHAPTER V

CHAPTER VI

CHAPTER VII

CHAPTER VIII

CHAPTER IX

CHAPTER X

JOHN MILTON

A Short Study of his Life and Works

PART I.—LIFE

CHAPTER I

EARLY YEARS (1608–1639)

THE fact that Milton was born in London on December 9, 1608, counts for not a little in his career. He was born early enough to catch much of the power and inspiration of the age of Elizabeth, but not early enough to catch its spirit of universal open-mindedness and free-heartedness. Thus it happens that some of the finest qualities of Shakspere, who epitomized the Elizabethans, are found in Milton in a state of arrested development,—for example, genial humor and, in a less degree, human sympathy. Had Milton been born twenty years earlier, it is possible that he might have surpassed Shakspere in totality of accomplishment, just as the latter surpassed Marlowe; for in point of grandeur, both of work and of character, the advantage seems to lie with Milton. Had his connections been even more entirely with the country instead of with the capital, the centre of political and religious activity, he might have lived his life under the spell of the Elizabethans, and left behind him poetical works more serenely, less strenuously artistic, than those we now possess, but also of wider range in point of underlying qualities. Yet these are might-have-beens, and some of us would not have Milton other than he is, — the greatest artist, man of letters, and ideal patriot, as we think, that the world has ever known. There are, however, certain points about his early career which are not at all hypothetical, and deserve careful though not, in this connection, minutely detailed attention.

He was the third child and namesake of a prosperous scrivener, of respectable family, whose puritanical leanings did not prevent him from conforming to the Established Church, from cultivating, with some success, the art of music, and from giving his children a broad education and a pleasant, happy home. From this father Milton probably inherited much of his genius, — a genius fostered by the wisdom and liberality of the parent to an extent that can scarcely be paralleled in our literary annals, save in the cases of Robert Browning and John Stuart Mill. That the youth was grateful is evidenced by his fine Latin verses, "Ad Patrem," especially by the lines: —

"Hoc utcumque tibi gratum, pater optime, carmen
Exiguum meditatur opus; nec novimus ipsi
Aptius a nobis quæ possint munera donis
Respondere tuis, quamvis nec maxima possint
Respondere tuis, nedum ut par gratia donis
Esse queat vacuis quæ redditur arida verbis."[1]

To his mother also, whose maiden name, Sarah Jeffrey, has been only recently ascertained, he owed not a little as every good man does, as well as to his early tutors with whom

[1] Thus rendered by Cowper: —

"For thee, my Father! howsoe'er it please,
She frames this slender work, nor know I aught
That may thy gifts more suitably requite;
Though to requite them suitably would ask
Returns much nobler, and surpassing far
The meagre stores of verbal gratitude."

he seems to have been on especially affectionate terms. One of these, Thomas Young, is still remembered by scholars as a Presbyterian controversialist of note, but his surest title to fame is found in these four lines of his pupil's: —

"Primus ego Aonios illo præeunte recessus
Lustrabam, et bifidi sacra vireta jugi,
Pieriosque hausi latices, Clioque favente
Castalio sparsi læta ter ora mero."[1]

Thus we see that the boy was grateful to his father and his teachers, and we have his subsequent testimony that he was so much in love with learning that from the early age of twelve he scarcely ever quit his lessons before midnight.[2] Yet there is nothing to show that then or afterward he was anything of a prig, and it is clear that he must have enjoyed and profited from his intercourse with the noted musi-

[1] Thus rendered by Cowper: —

"First led by him through sweet Aonian shade,
Each sacred haunt of Pindus I survey'd;
And favored by the muse, whom I implored,
Thrice on my lip the hallow'd stream I pour'd."

[2] See the long and fine autobiographical passage in the "Second Defence" — the source of much of our best information about Milton.

cians that frequented his father's house. The phrase so loosely used by us, a liberal education, applies in full force to Milton — his was the education given by good training, by contact with ripe minds and with sound learning, and by practice in the liberalizing art of music. Nor was that finer element of a well-spent youth, friendship with a companion of the same age and sex, lacking to him. His intimacy with Charles Diodati, the son of an Italian physician settled in London for religious reasons, left its mark, we cannot doubt, on Milton's character as well as upon his Latin verses. Diodati's devotion has been repaid by the "Epitaphium Damonis," but Milton's has not been sufficiently remembered by those who insist that he was practically devoid of the intimate human sympathies. No man destitute of such sympathies could have written such poetry as Milton's, but it is fair to say that the direct influence of his fellows counted for less with him than with any other great world poet. Yet he is also the sublimest, though not the most universal of the poets, and perhaps in his case and always, sublime elevation is obtained only through isolation. Be this as it may, the indirect influence of men through their books counted for more with Milton than can be estimated in words. From his earliest youth he was not merely an earnest student but an unsatiated reader, and to this day he stands as our most learned poet and cultured artist, Ben Jonson not excepted.

About 1620 Milton entered St. Paul's School as a day-scholar and remained there until 1625, when he commenced residence, during the Easter term, at Christ's College, Cambridge. At school he profited from the acquirements, both in the classics and in the vernacular, of the head-master Dr. Alexander Gill, and somewhat from the friendship of the latter's able but rather graceless son, namesake, and assistant. Here, too, he formed his friendship with Diodati and began his apprenticeship as a poet by paraphrases of Psalms cxiv. and cxxxvi.—exercises which, if reminiscential of the work of other poets, nevertheless deserve the praise of Dr. Garnett as being in general tone both "masculine and emphatic."

Why his father should have selected Cambridge for him is uncertain, but it is quite clear that although Milton continued his university studies for seven years, taking his B.A. in 1629 and his M.A. in 1632, he did not enter into the spirit of the place. He tells us in one of his controversial tracts that he "never greatly admired" it in his youth, and one of his Latin academical exercises lets us see that he probably indulged in strictures on the methods of instruction. From the elaborate account of the Cambridge of the time put together by Professor Masson one is inclined to infer that the studious and well-trained undergraduate had reason for his criticisms. There were able men among the instructors, but none capable of arousing the enthusiasm of a self-contained youth like Milton; and although the poet John Cleveland, and Henry More, the Platonist, were members of his college, they were his juniors in age and standing. Yet we have Milton's word for it that the fellows of Christ's treated him with "more than ordinary respect," and we know that he was several times accorded the honor of selection as a public speaker. As for the story that he was actually whipped by his unsympathetic tutor, William Chappell, a tool of Laud's, we may dismiss it as an idle tale, or else as a distorted version of a personal encounter between pupil and instructor. Nevertheless the fact remains clear that Milton heads the list of great English men of letters who have been out of sympathy with their universities — a list that includes Dryden and Gibbon and Shelley and Byron.

Yet during these college years he was laying the broad foundations of his character and his culture. The personal purity preserved through all temptation and ridicule (his fellow-students dubbed him "Lady" as much on this account, we cannot doubt, as because of his conspicuous beauty of face and figure), enabled him to expound as no other poet has ever done

> "the sage
> And serious doctrine of Virginity;"

the self-absorption in the pursuit of high ideals, the proud aloofness from common things and common men that characterized him, may have lessened his human sympathies, but assuredly made possible that supremely ideal love of religion and his native land that prompted and accomplished as noble a deed of patriotic self-sacrifice as has yet been recorded to the credit of the race; and finally it is hard to believe that he would ever have become master of so profound and exact an erudition and so serene and balanced a culture, had he not profited by that systematic training and discipline of the faculties which is imparted in full measure by a historic university alone. It should be remembered furthermore that during his university career he found time and inspiration to write much of his Latin verse, as well as such great English poems as the ode "On the Morning of Christ's Nativity," the epitaph "On Shakspere," and the sonnet "On his being arrived at the age of twenty-three." This was no slight achievement in verse, especially if we add two serious and good elegies, two humorous ones, two fragments, and perhaps the exquisite "Song on May Morning"; but more important was the formation of the resolution to which he ever afterward adhered — to order his life

"As ever in *his* great Task-Master's eye."

When he left Cambridge he betook himself to his father's halfway suburban residence at Horton, in Buckinghamshire. Although he had criticised the administration of the university, he seems to have been pressed to take a fellowship, but that would have meant practically taking orders; and while such had once been his intention, he felt now that he could not conscientiously pursue the latter course. The church service could not have been very irksome to him, for he had borne it daily for seven years; nor could theological difficulties have beset him greatly, for he subscribed the Articles on taking his degree, and his Arian proclivities were a matter of later years. It was at the ecclesiastical organization then controlled by Laud, who was fostering to the best of his abilities and in a peculiarly exasperating way the high-church reaction, that the Puritan idealist looked askance. He would not "subscribe slave" even though he were conscious that with his scholarly tastes he would find it hard to discover a better profession. He preferred to be "church-outed by the prelates" and was nobly serious if also somewhat stiff-necked about it. Had he continued at Cambridge he would assuredly have been the centre of many an academic dispute; it is impossible to say what would have happened had he entered the Church in any active way and been brought into personal contact with Laud. He would have gone down temporarily before bigotry in power; but the genius even of a Boswell would have failed to do justice to an encounter that would have required a Shakspere.

If Milton read his own character as we now do, and restrained his ardent nature that he might allow his powers to ripen through solitude and study, he more than deserves the epithets he bestowed upon his favorite Spenser — "sage and serious." If he did not fully understand himself, but simply felt conscious of high powers and a mission to fulfil, he deserves all the praise that belongs so amply to those "who only stand and wait." But much praise is due to the father also who, now that his active life was over and his chief interests were necessarily centred in the success of his children, was content to do his share of waiting till the genius of his son should, in the fulness of time, become manifest to the world. That genius was slowly developing itself through study, contemplation, intercourse with nature, and occasional wooing of the muse. He mastered the ancient classics and the chief writers of more recent times until he may be said to have lived with them. He contemplated life with all its possibilities, and became more firmly fixed in his determination to devote himself to the service of humanity, to lead a life that should be a true poem, and to leave behind him some child of his imagination that posterity would not willingly let die. He watched, too, with poignant anguish the headlong course of Charles and Laud, toward destruction, and saw that they would involve in ruin not merely themselves and the Church, but the nation for which he already felt the burning passion of the man who not loving easily, loves the more deeply. But he contemplated also the serene beauty of the peaceful landscape around him, and the spirit of nature took hold upon him — not as it had done on Shakspere and was to do on Wordsworth and Byron — but in a true, noble, and powerful way. Finally he wrote verse to relieve his pent-up feelings or to oblige friends, yet never without keeping his eyes fixed on the masters of his craft and registering a solemn vow not to allow himself to be tempted by easy praise to abandon the arduous upward path on which his feet were set. It is to the five years (1632–1637) spent at Horton that we are said to owe "L'Allegro," "Il Penseroso," "Arcades," "Comus," and "Lycidas" — poems so perfect that many critics laying aside their judgment, which must always consider quantity as well as quality of work, have actually regarded them as the most adequate expression of Milton's poetical genius. This they are not if the sublime in art be accorded its true supremacy, yet they are at once so strong and so exquisite that the fact that they were composed at Horton should make the little Buckinghamshire village second only to Stratford in interest to all lovers of English poetry.[1]

[1] Milton tells us that he paid occasional visits to London to purchase books or to learn something new in *mathematics* or music. ("Second Defence.")

In the spring of 1638 Milton undertook to put the finishing touch upon his education by setting out for Italy. The spell that that fair but fatally dowered land exercises on every liberal soul, had already been communicated to him through the medium of her great poets, but it was not to be sealed permanently upon his spirit as it has been since upon Byron, Shelley, Landor, and Browning. He was fitter than these to penetrate into Italy's secret, being the most artistic spirit England has ever borne, and it is interesting to speculate what a longer residence under the sky that smiles upon Naples and Florence and Venice would have meant for him; but that was not to be. Yet we may be sure that no nobler stranger has ever since apostolic times set foot upon that sacred soil so often trod by alien feet — not Chaucer or Goethe, not Luther or Bayard. Shakspere probably never saw the land that his genius so often adorned, and Dante was its native — and it is with Shakspere and Dante alone of all moderns that we may fittingly compare Milton.

The details of his journey are scant, but even

the few facts we know must be given rapidly here. Stopping for a brief space at Paris, he met Grotius, and then proceeded by Nice, Genoa, Leghorn, and Pisa, to Florence. Here he was introduced to the most cultured representatives of that day of Italy's decline, and frequented their academies, and paid as good Latin compliments as he received. He impressed all who met him by his beauty, his grace, his mental and spiritual attainments, and if the tributes paid him were extravagant, they nevertheless retain even to this day a note of sincerity. We do not know whether the sightless Galileo thought him an angel or an Angle, but it is easy to agree with Dr. Garnett that—"the meeting between the two great blind men of their century is one of the most picturesque in history; it would have been more pathetic still if Galileo could have known that his name would be written in 'Paradise Lost,' or Milton could have foreseen that within thirteen years he too would see only with the inner eye, but that the calamity which disabled the astronomer would restore inspiration to the poet."

From Florence Milton went, via Siena, to Rome, where he remained two months, and was treated with consideration in spite of his imprudent habit of discussing religious matters in public. He was fascinated by the singing of Leonora Baroni, on whom he wrote three Latin epigrams, but he is silent, so critics have observed, about the effects of antiquity and of modern plastic art upon his spirit.[1] His natural aptitude was for music, and perhaps when later, his Puritan controversies put by, he took up poetry once more, his loss of sight inclined him to leave unsung the glories of arts he could no longer appreciate. It was different with nature, whose effects he could still feel and whose beauty he was bound by the scheme of his work to describe.

Naples was the next stage of his journey, and there tidings reached him of the distracted political state of his native land. He gave up at once his intention of proceeding to Sicily and Greece, but was leisurely enough in his return. He again spent two months at Rome

[1] He tells us expressly that he viewed the antiquities of Rome, and the company of Lucas Holstein, the Vatican librarian, and other scholars would indicate that he did not waste his time.

and an equal period at Florence, barring a visit to Lucca, and proceeded to Venice by way of Bologna, where an Italian lady is said to have fascinated him. The sonnets written in her native language lend some color to this statement, which would at least furnish additional proof of Milton's lack of essential English narrowness; but the whole affair is shadowy, and the sonnets may have been mere exercises in a strange tongue. It is better perhaps to lay stress on the actual friendship formed at Naples with the venerable Marquis Manso, the protector of Tasso and Marini, and upon the noble Latin verses in which Milton repaid the generosity of his host and announced his own hope of some day acquiring perennial fame through an epic upon King Arthur and his Table Round. It would be too painful to lay stress upon the anguish of his spirit when he reached Geneva from Venice, via Verona and Milan, and there probably heard for the first time of the death of the friend of his boyhood and of his riper years, the man who had first brought him in touch with the beautiful land he was just leaving, — Charles Diodati.

CHAPTER II

THE MAN OF AFFAIRS (1640-1660)

MILTON once more set foot on English soil toward the end of July, 1639. His first act of any moment was one of piety. He wrote his greatest and practically his last Latin poem, the "Epitaphium Damonis," in honor of Diodati — a tribute the exquisite sincerity of which its foreign medium of expression cannot impair, but unfortunately obscures to those of his race whose classical education has been neglected. It was also, with the exception of a pair of sonnets, to be the last of his elegiac poems, for his father's death eight years later, just as his mother's, two years previously, called forth no poetical expression of grief. For Diodati, the returned traveller could not but mourn in the language in which they had exchanged their innermost feelings, and which linked them both with the land from which one sprang and to which the other was still turning regretful eyes.

His elegy finished, he set himself to a less congenial but in every way honorable task — he began to teach his two nephews, Edward and John Phillips, sons of his elder sister Anne, now a Mrs. Agar. He lived at first in lodgings, his younger brother Christopher continuing to reside with their father at Horton; but in a short time he found it convenient to take a house in the somewhat suburban Aldersgate Street. Here he taught his pupils and watched the course of public events.

Milton as a schoolmaster may suggest to some the veriest profanation of genius, to others that irony of fate at which we smile or jest; but no one who has read the tractate entitled "Of Education," or rightly gauged the poet's character, or comprehended the true dignity of the teacher's office, will ever regret the quiet months devoted to pedagogical pursuits and the "intermitted studies." So, too, no one not a hopeless partisan of the Stuarts, or biassed like Mark Pattison in favor of the scholarly life, will regret that Milton took interest enough in public affairs to smile at Charles's failure to subdue Scotland and to wait eagerly for the Long Parliament to throw open the doors concealing "that two-handed engine."

But neither teaching nor politics, we may be sure, seemed to him at that time worthy of being made his permanent vocation. His note-books prove, as we shall see later, that he was meditating deeply upon the great poem he felt called upon to write. He was preparing to be a *vates*, when circumstances determined that he should become, not a dictator, but a dictator's spokesman and champion. For twenty years he wrote no verse save a comparatively small number of sonnets, and his silence during a period when most poets do their best work might easily have resulted in England's having only one supreme poet instead of two. But Providence willed otherwise, and our shudder at the risk our literature ran should not make us forget the fact that to Milton's participation in politics we owe not only the most magnificently sonorous prose ever written by an Englishman, but also much of the force and nobility of "Paradise Lost" itself.[1]

It was the resolute spirit shown by the Long Parliament in its early days, especially with regard to ecclesiastical grievances, that plunged Milton into politics with the resolve "to transfer into this struggle all *his* genius and all the strength of *his* industry." The humbling of Charles, the arrest and imprisonment of Laud, and the execution of Strafford had shown the religious and political reformers their power, and had brought into prominence not merely men of action, but also a crowd of zealous and advanced theorists, and of visionary schemers for the ordering of Church and State. It is always so with revolutions. The French had their Abbé Siéyès, and we Americans had scores of theorists from Jefferson down. But no such ideal reformer as Milton has ever since lifted his voice above the din of faction, and if we convict him of partisanship, we must nevertheless figure him to ourselves as a seraphic partisan. To fail to do

[1] See Dr. Garnett's admirable remarks on this subject, "Life of Milton," pp. 68, 69.

this is to fail to comprehend one of the most inspiring characters in all history, yet thousands have so failed because they could not forgive certain coarse expressions characteristic of the times and circumstances or because they were not capable of acknowledging greatness in a political or religious opponent. Milton's fame has suffered from their alienation, yet surely their loss has been the greater, for not to know and love the sublimest of all human idealists is an inestimable misfortune. That such is Milton's transcendent position cannot, of course, be proved, but it is perhaps admissible for an admirer to believe that no man ever got to the heart of the master's writings without being convinced of the truth of the statement.

Milton's first utterances were naturally on the subject of episcopacy, the abolition of which had been proposed in the Commons, and as naturally they took the form of rather cumbrous pamphlets. To some critics it is now difficult not merely to see any force in his arguments, but even to comprehend at all the point of view maintained by him in the five tractates of 1641–42. Minute study of them will convince us, however, of Milton's grasp of the situation, of his logical power, and of his essential purity of mind and heart. It was not to him a question of expediency that he was considering; it was a question whether God or the Devil should rule in England, if not in the world. The sublime confidence with which he promulgated his ideas of Church polity moves our wonder; the impassioned language in which he clothed those ideas moves not only our admiration but a sense of our infinite inferiority. Such swelling periods of prophecy and denunciation, of high purpose and holy hope, have been possible to one man alone — to the future author of "Paradise Lost." Whether or not we love Laud less and Milton more, whether or not we seek the arena of religious controversy, we cannot but conclude that the crisis which called forth the dithyrambic close of the tract entitled "Of Reformation in England" was not lacking in momentous results to England's literature and to the character and work of her noblest son.

The outbreak of war in the autumn of 1642 forced upon Milton the question whether he should take up arms in defence of the principles he advocated. We know his exact course of reasoning, and thus need not infer it. He could serve his country and his God better with his pen than with his sword, so instead of fighting, he wrote his sonnet "When the Assault was Intended to the City"—that superb plea for the inviolability of the "Muse's bower." To blame Milton for not becoming a soldier is like blaming Washington for not writing an epic on the Revolutionary War after he had sheathed his sword. The man whose imagination was already revolving the war in heaven, was not wanted on the fields of Naseby and Dunbar: the prophet of the glories of a renovated and redeemed England had faith enough to believe that God would, in due season, show forth the man who should render those glories possible. He could not foresee that the representatives of the people for whom he sang and Cromwell fought would one day refuse the meed of a statue to their greatest ruler and soldier; but could he rise from the dead he would set the seal of his approval upon the fiery protest against a nation's ingratitude recently wrung from a poet into whom he has breathed not a little of his own impassioned eloquence and love of liberty: —

"The enthroned Republic from her kinglier throne
Spake, and her speech was Cromwell's. Earth has known
No lordlier presence. How should Cromwell stand
By kinglets and by queenlings hewn in stone?"[1]

But while Oxford was protesting her loyalty and Cornwall was rising in arms and the king's cause seemed by no means hopeless, Milton, for the first time in his life apparently,[2] was falling seriously in love. Exactly how this came about is not known. He seems to have gone to Oxfordshire in the spring of 1643 to collect a debt from a Cavalier squire, Richard Powell by name, and to have returned to London in a month with this gentleman's daughter, Mary, as his bride. A party of her

[1] A. C. Swinburne in *The Nineteenth Century* for July, 1895. The Conservative government has since accepted as a *gift* the bust by Bernini.

[2] Unless we believe in the Bolognese love affair.

relatives soon after visited the pair, and the young wife appears to have enjoyed their dancing more than she did her husband's philosophizing, for she shortly after left him under promise of return and took up her abode with her father, from whose protection she could not be induced to withdraw, in spite of Milton's protestations, until about two years had elapsed.

As a matter of course this marriage venture of Milton's — the most mysterious, perhaps, in history save that of Sam Houston, the hero of San Jacinto — has been much discussed, and Mary Powell has found stanch advocates in inveterate maligners of her husband. An additional element of disturbance was unwittingly contributed to the controversy by Professor Masson when he discovered that in all likelihood the first edition of Milton's pamphlet on "The Doctrine and Discipline of Divorce," was issued on August 1, 1643, *i.e.* a little after or just about the time of his wife's departure for her father's house. It had been previously believed that Edward Phillips's statement that the tract was written after Mary Milton's positive refusal to return to her husband was correct, but now this seems to apply only to the second and enlarged edition of the following February. Yet what sort of man was this who could argue in cold blood during his honeymoon about the justice of allowing divorce for incompatibility of temperament!

Milton's foes would have his friends on the hip if he had actually argued in cold blood; but that was very far from Milton's way of arguing anything. As Dr. Garnett has deftly shown, the first edition of the "Doctrine and Discipline" was not only highly idealistic but profoundly emotional, and was just the sort of protest against his fate that might have been wrung from an intense, proud-spirited man like Milton in the days that followed his wife's departure. The second edition was his reasoned plea, though it too was full of emotion; the first was the almost lyrical outburst of his deeply tried soul struggling for escape. If any one will read the noble preface, "To the Parliament of England, with the Assembly," he will be forced to confess that, whatever were Milton's domestic reasons for writing, he nevertheless wrote in all honesty, and speedily passed from a consideration of his own case to an impassioned plea for reform in the interests of the common weal. His resolutions were "firmly seated in a square and constant mind, not conscious to itself of any deserved blame, and regardless of ungrounded suspicions." He could proudly and sincerely say, "I have already my greatest gain, assurance, and inward satisfaction to have done in this nothing unworthy of an honest life and studies well employed." He could actually compare his new light on the subject of divorce with the gospel preached upon the continent by Willibrod and Winifrid, and conclude with that noblest of sentiments — "Let not England forget her precedence of teaching nations how to live."

Milton's tract was therefore sincere and characteristic of him, but this is not a proof that it was a worthy thing to write and publish. Yet perhaps if we will read his utterances carefully and remember that he wrote at a time when every liberal mind was narrowly examining the structure of society and projecting discoveries and applications of new moral and political truths, we shall come to the conclusion that he acted not only consistently, but worthily, with regard to this whole divorce matter. If we condemn him merely because our views on the question of divorce are stricter than his, — our ideal of a true marriage could not be higher, — we have just as much right to condemn him for his ultra-puritanism or his ultra-republicanism — that is, we have no right to condemn him at all, for we are obviously called upon to judge him now only as a man and a great creative writer, not as a theorist in religion and politics.

But can Milton be absolved of blame as a man for his treatment of his first wife? One may answer, "Yes, so far as the evidence goes." His demands upon the girl were probably excessive, but then he was an idealist who had somehow made a bad match. If she suffered, so did he; and the chances are a thousand to one against the grave, dignified man's having wantonly offended his young wife, while they are not nearly so great against the shallow Royalist girl's having uttered light and flippant gibes about her Puritan husband's noblest and dearest ideals. As to Milton's alleged attentions to the "very handsome and witty" daughter of Dr. Davis, one can only say that, in view of Milton's sincerity and courage of character, they are an additional proof of his determination to announce his principles and act upon them. The young lady and her parents were probably able to look out for themselves and must have shared Milton's ideals, or, in view of the danger attending the woman from the state of the law, he would have been asked to cease his visits. To blame him for being "light of love" is simply to forget that strong natures bent in one direction rebound far when released. Perhaps Mistress Davis's qualities were complementary to those of Mary Powell, or perhaps gossips mistook a Platonic friendship for a love affair. Be this as it may, we know that in July or August, 1645, the wife surprised the husband at a friend's house, and that a reconciliation was effected. Perhaps, as has been urged, she was brought to terms by the visits to Mistress Davis; but on the face of things her voluntary return is a circumstance in Milton's favor.

This is not the place to discuss in detail the divorce pamphlets which proved too strong a diet even for Milton's coreligionists and had to be published without license — a fact to which we owe the greatest and best known of his prose writings, the noble "Areopagitica, a Speech for the Liberty of Unlicensed Printing." But before the thread of his married life is taken up once more, it will be well to say a few words about his relations with women in general. He has been much criticised for them, not always with entire justice. If he did not enjoy much happiness with his first wife, he could nevertheless write his noble sonnet to his second, Katherine Woodcock,[1] a sufficient tribute to any woman, though perhaps borrowed in substance from a similar sonnet by the Italian poet, Bernadino Rota; while with his third wife, Elizabeth Minshull,

[1] The second marriage lasted from November, 1656, to February, 1658. The marriage for convenience with the "genteel" Mistress Minshull took place in 1663.

who survived him, he seems to have lived as congenially as could be expected when all the circumstances are taken into account. His daughters by his first wife have won a sympathy which they scarcely deserve. Reading aloud in languages one does not understand is not an enjoyable task; but what are we to say of the characters and dispositions of women who could lack reverence for such a father? Admiration and sympathy are two of the noblest attributes of womanhood, and who has ever been fitter to elicit them than Milton in his blindness? Perhaps the best excuse for these daughters is the fact that they were trained in part by their mother. We may dismiss this unpleasant topic with the remark that it is well to note that in the scanty tale of Milton's English sonnets there are four addressed to women in which there is not a line to make us believe that he had a low estimate of the sex, and much to convince us, in spite of the often-quoted lines of "Paradise Lost" which represent the normal view of the period, that he was at times capable of extending to them that intelligent admiration which the mass of mankind are only just beginning to recognize as their due. This conviction is rendered almost a certainty when we study the relations of the poet with the famous Lady Ranelagh, the learned and virtuous Katherine Boyle, mother of "the noble youth, Richard Jones," whom Milton taught and to whom he indited some epistles. It will probably be impossible to root from the public mind the notion that Milton was a sour woman-hater and a vindictive partisan, but we may be sure that the records do not warrant any such conception of his character, and we should protest emphatically against such an egregious assumption as that of Professor Dowden to the effect that there is an unlovely Milton from whom we are all anxious to avert our gaze.

Early in 1646, at the solicitation of Humphrey Moseley, the publisher, who seems to have known what a favor he was doing mankind, Milton, who, except in the cases of his *magnum opus* and "Samson Agonistes," generally waited for an external stimulus to literary undertakings, brought out the first edition of his poems in two parts, English and Latin.

He prefixed a quotation from Virgil which showed that he regarded the publication as premature. In view of the great praise now given to the minor poems, this attitude of Milton's might seem to furnish fresh evidence of the irony attaching to the judgments of authors about their own works; but if we can appreciate duly the transcendent merits of "Paradise Lost" and will remember that the scheme of that noble work was even then occupying Milton's thoughts, his unwillingness to rush into print will smack neither of the irony of self-judgment nor of false modesty. Be this as it may, it was an unpropitious time for the muses that he or his publisher chose; but it was not many years before he was plagiarized from in a shocking manner by one Robert Barron, and if imitation be the sincerest flattery, he ought to have been pleased, but probably was not. Meanwhile his school had increased, and he had moved into larger quarters, whither his wife's relatives, who had been dispossessed by the Parliamentarians, presently flocked in a way to make one suspect that they had had a reason for helping to bring husband and wife together once more. Milton seems to have done his duty by them in an exemplary manner, and he obviously deserves far more sympathy than he has ever got. They inspired little poetry, we may be sure, but he worked away at his studies, gathered materials for his "History of England," and perhaps began his treatise "De Doctrina Christiana," which through a train of curious circumstances did not see the light until 1823. In 1647 his father, who had been living with him since the lapsing of Christopher Milton to royalism and Roman Catholicism, died, and the consequent addition to his income led him to give up all his pupils, save his nephews. He also moved to a smaller house and got rid of the daily presence of the Powells. So he lived on and looked out at the swift succession of events that seemed about to change entirely the course of English history. He was still conscious of great powers and still yearning for an opportunity to do something for his people, but he preferred a scholarly seclusion, as he tells us, to a station "at the doors of the court with a petitioner's face."

With the king's death, however, a change

took place in Milton's affairs. Charles was beheaded on January 30, 1649; in exactly two weeks Milton had published his pamphlet "The Tenure of Kings and Magistrates," in which he maintained the right of "any who have the Power, to call to account a Tyrant, or wicked King, and after due Conviction, to depose, and put him to Death, if the ordinary Magistrate have neglected, or denied to do it." This was a bold and certainly expeditious defence of the actions of his party — how bold may be somewhat realized when we remember how the news of the execution of Louis XVI., nearly a century and a half later, resounded through Europe. Even the philosophic mind of Burke was unhinged by the latter catastrophe; the former and more astounding event simply woke Milton up. Merely as a private citizen with convictions of his own and as an enthusiast whose dash for the breach showed him to be uninfluenced by political or other calculations, he dared to defend a deed which had filled a whole people with horror and consternation; to the seductions of sympathy stimulated by the timely appearance of the "Eikon Basilike," he opposed the warning voice of reason and the high, clear strains of duty. If he took an untenable position in some particulars, he nevertheless put the half-hearted to shame and enrolled his own name high among the sons of liberty. The popular leaders could overlook him no longer, and he was offered the post of Latin Secretary to the Committee on Foreign Affairs. The salary was ample,—about $5250 in our present money,—and the position such as even a Milton could accept, for he was not merely to carry on diplomatic correspondence in the language of scholars, but also to be the recognized spokesman of his party. In his own eyes it was the spokesman of liberty and his native land that he aspired to be, and the proffered office gave him an opportunity of realizing his aspiration. There could be little or no thought of a refusal, and he thus became, as Dr. Garnett happily puts it, "the Orpheus among the Argonauts of the Commonwealth."

His first work as Secretary that need be noticed here was his "Eikonoklastes," written in answer to the "Eikon Basilike" of Bishop Gauden, then generally believed to be the work of the "Royal Martyr" himself. Milton seems to have shirked the task, knowing that to accomplish it effectively would necessitate depreciation of the dead king and much chaffering over straws. In spite of this known reluctance on his part and of the obvious fact that much of his matter and manner was determined by the nature and arrangement of the treatise he was answering, critics have not ceased to search his book minutely for data on which to rest charges against his personal integrity, his consistency, even his taste in literature. But he was soon to undertake a greater task, and one that was to bring him more fame, since he did little with "Eikonoklastes" to stem the tide in favor of the pseudo-religious martyr. The learned Frenchman, Claude de Saumaise, better known as Salmasius, the discoverer of the Palatine Ms. of the Greek Anthology, had been employed to unmask the batteries of his ponderous erudition, so valued at the time, in defence of Charles I. His "Defensio Regia" appeared in the latter part of 1649, and Milton was directed by the Council to answer it. He did at the cost of his sight. For some years his eyes had been failing, and one was already gone. He was advised that any further strain would speedily induce total blindness, yet he never wavered in the performance of his duty. He calmly faced the loss of a sense that every true scholar must value more than life itself; he put from him all anticipation of the noble pleasure he had looked forward to deriving from the first sight of his great poem in print; he may even have despaired of ever composing the poem at all; he looked forward to the miseries of a cheerless old age, and without repining accepted a commission that could not under any circumstances have been specially grateful to him — all because he deemed it right that his country and party should make a proper reply to the charges that had been laid against them in the forum of European opinion. If a sublimer act of patriotic self-sacrifice has ever been performed, it has surely never been recorded. And yet readers have been found who could calmly dissect the "Pro Populo Anglicano Defensio contra Salmasium" and argue from it that its author had not merely a bad cause, but a bad temper and a worse taste. There have been critics who have imagined that it is proper to judge a seventeenth century controversialist by standards more talked about than acted upon in the nineteenth. There have even been friends of Milton who, forgetting that the man is and ought to be greater than the poet, have wished that he had never performed this act of self-sacrifice that makes him the true Milton of song and history.

And now by the spring of 1652 the Milton who had won the plaudits of cultivated Italians for his beauty and his grace, the Milton who had looked on nature's face and found her fair, the Milton who had at last been brought to mingle with the affairs of men at a critical juncture in his country's history, was totally blind, an object of pity, a man who was apparently without a future. It was due to the fact that he was Milton and no one else that he did not succumb but became the poet of "Paradise Lost." And as if to complete his misfortunes, the death of his wife left him the blind father of three little girls. Under such circumstances he can have thought little of his sudden leap into European fame through the complete victory he had gained over Salmasius. That victory, like all partisan victories, was dearly bought, for the price paid was nothing less than the consciousness that he was execrated by hundreds of thousands of his fellow-countrymen.

The literary duel which cost Milton his sight and Salmasius his life, according to the doubtless exaggerated story, was followed by a sorry squabble which would be regrettable but for the fact that it led Milton to make certain autobiographical confessions of great value. A scurrilous tract was written against him by a broken-down parson, Peter du Moulin by name, who managed to keep his identity well concealed. Milton was led by plausible reasons to believe that his reviler was one Alexander Morus, a Scoto-Frenchman, pastor and professor of Sacred History at Amsterdam, and a resident in Salmasius's household, in which he did not conduct himself with perfect chastity. Morus, hearing that Milton was contemplating a reply to the anonymous pamphlet, and fearing the weight of his hand, hastened to assert his innocence in the affair. Milton would listen to nothing, however, and published his reply in 1654. Then Morus was literally flogged into taking up whatever literary weapons he could find, but Milton crushed him with another tract the following year. We shall refer to these productions again, but we must confess here that nothing connected with Milton's life is less edifying. It should be remembered, however, that no man, not even a Milton, can be expected to be far in advance of his times in his methods of personal controversy, and that controversy was a prime constituent of the intellectual atmosphere of the seventeenth century.

Milton's State Papers are less disquieting reading than his controversial fulminations. It seems quite clear that while he was but carrying out the wishes and plans of his superiors in office he threw into his letters to foreign potentates not a little of his own noble spirit. Whether he was able, even before he lost his sight, to affect the policy of Cromwell, which he certainly ventured to criticise, is very doubtful; but he was none the less the spokesman of his party while living, and he has ever since been its articulate voice. Perhaps it is just as well that in revolving in imagination those eventful years of English history we should not confuse the two dominant conceptions that come to us — that we should always be able to distinguish Cromwell's vigor and Milton's godlike utterance.

The blind man's utterance was in some respects more potent than the Protector's vigor, for the latter could not be transmitted to Richard Cromwell or to any other survivor, while Milton could and did continue to inculcate his lofty conceptions of the true nature of Church and State. His blindness and his enforced confinement to his home and the companionship of a few choice friends like Andrew Marvell, his assistant secretary, and the Cyriack Skinner and Henry Lawrence of the sonnets, doubtless proved to him a blessing in disguise, for he could not see how the fabric of popular government was rushing to its fall. He heard enough to disquiet him, and he doubtless brooded over what he heard, but his practical withdrawal from the world must have deadened the shock of the Restoration and rendered less vivid his solicitude as to his own fate. To those, however, who have studied the shameful history of England for the year 1659, the isolation of the blind poet but adds to the pathos of the picture he presents — a Republican Samson, captive in the midst of his contemptible foes. Yet even the pathos of this picture should not make us wish with Mark Pattison that Milton had never sunk the poet in the man of affairs. It seems as idle to argue that "Paradise Lost" would have been the poem it is without the poetic interregnum of 1640–1660, as it is to argue that Milton would have been as great a man without it. Those critics may indeed be right who maintain that Milton's nature was subdued to what it worked in, "like the dyer's hand," that the Puritan controversialist sometimes got the better of the poet long after occasion for controversy had passed away (as if Milton could ever have thought this!)—but such criticism means merely that Milton had not the universality of genius, the absolute perfection of artistic balance that characterize Homer, and perhaps Shakspere, alone of the world's poets. No one has ever claimed such universality, such perfect balance for him; his sublime elevation of consummate nobility being sufficient basis for his eternal fame.

CHAPTER III

THE SUPREME POET (1661–1674)

It is easy enough to infer that Milton did not fully understand the signs of the times from the fact that he published two of his idealistic political and theological tracts in 1659, and one, the "Ready and Easy Way to Establish a Free Commonwealth," not two months before Charles II. reëntered his kingdom. If he had understood the times thoroughly, and perceived of what gross clay his fellow-countrymen were made, he would hardly have had the spirit to pen his eloquent periods. Yet he knew more or less what was coming, and he displayed his matchless courage in protesting the justice of Charles I.'s execution on the eve of the triumphal advent of Charles II. He was not foolhardy, however, for early in May he left his house and went into hiding in Bartholomew Close, Smithfield.

If either king or Parliament had been bloody-minded, Milton would almost certainly have been brought to the scaffold. His writings were burned by the hangman on August 27, but influential friends made it possible for his name to be omitted from the list of twenty persons who were proscribed in addition to the authentic regicides. He actually escaped arrest for a long while, and when this came, suffered only from the exaction of heavy fees. Finally he found a refuge in Holborn, his nerves shaken, and his property greatly reduced, partly in consequence of his political affiliations. There is nothing more pathetic in history than this return of Milton to the outer world. Blind, reviled, despised by his own children, his ideals shattered, his health impaired, he had but one comfort, — his undefiled conscience; and but one hope, — the completion of the great poem he had already begun.

But by degrees his condition began to mend. His third marriage restored order to his home and prevented his daughters from selling his books. His friends visited him faithfully, and his organ was a source of unfailing pleasure.

Readers and amanuenses were provided, and the labor of composition went on, interrupted only by his own singular inaptitude for work at certain seasons. By 1663, five years after its inception, the first draft of the immortal epic was probably completed; in two years more it was in all likelihood fit for the printer; but the fatal Plague and Fire doubtless impeded business negotiations, and certainly sent the poet down to Chalfont St. Giles, where the interesting Quaker, Thomas Ellwood, visited him and asked the famous question which probably led to the composition of "Paradise Regained." Before, however, the latter poem was published along with "Samson Agonistes" in 1671, the greatest epic since "The Divine Comedy" had passed so as by fire through the sapient hands of the licenser, the Reverend Thomas Tomkyns, and had been printed by Samuel Simmons (in 1667) on terms that have been made the subject of many critical homilies.

Mr. Simmons may have driven a hard bargain, though there is much room to doubt it; but he did better by Milton and his epic than a good many modern critics have done who are not supposed to hold chairs in the School of Cobbett. We are told now that people do not read "Paradise Lost," and that its subject is antiquated and a little absurd, especially since the theory of evolution has thrown grave doubts upon the lion's ever having pawed to extricate his hinder parts. If this be true of the public, and if our critics are to judge poets from the point of view of Cobbett's so-called common sense or of Huxley's epoch-making science, it may well be doubted whether printer Simmons was not more a child of the muses than one is likely to jostle to-day on the streets of any of our great cities. But Simmons's niggardly pounds have either been quite worn out or have forgotten that they ever took part in a prudent or a shabby transaction, and a similar fate awaits the Cobbett critics and the public that pays attention to them. "Paradise Lost" has set a seal upon Milton's glory that can be effaced or unloosed by angelic power alone — by the might of the angel who shall in the fulness of time blow the last trump.

With regard to the pendant epic and the noble drama in classical style whose date of composition is uncertain, little need be said here save that those persons who refrain from reading them stand greatly in their own light. Neither can claim the preëminence in our poetry that belongs of right to "Paradise Lost," but none the less both poems are worthy of Milton, and therefore of our admiration and love. They may give evidence of the declining powers of his mighty genius, or they may, more probably, represent that genius moving in regions less elevated and pure; but they are worthy to shine through their own lustre, and to live through their own vitality. Their comparative unpopularity is proof of nothing save of the proverbial isolation of the noble; but their existence is proof of the fact that in a blind old age Milton would be content with nothing less than a strenuous and lofty use of his divinely bestowed powers. He could not, like his Nazarene hero, pull down the pillars of an ungodly state upon the heads of its citizens, although he would not have shirked the self-destruction involved; but he could still sing in exultant tones of the triumphs of virtue and of the justice and majesty and mercy of God.

That mercy was shown him in his last years in fuller measure than he perhaps expected, or than his political and ecclesiastical foes would have admitted to be his due. He was passed by in ignorance or contempt by the great world; but here and there a judicious celebrity like Dryden would pay his court to him, and the old friends remained faithful. The gout afflicted him, but not enough to keep him from singing. He had the pleasure of utilizing manuscripts prepared in better days, and of thus discharging his debt toward posterity with the utmost punctiliousness. The small Latin grammar (1669), the "History of Britain" (1670), the "Art of Logic" (1672), the tract on "True Religion, Heresy, Schism, Toleration" (1673), the revised and enlarged edition of the "Minor Poems" (1673), the "Familiar Epistles" (in Latin, 1674), is a catalogue of undertakings of no transcendent moment, but amply sufficient to prove that Milton did not pass many completely idle days. His political and diplomatic correspondence and his treatise on "Christian Doctrine" could not of course see the light then, but the latter at least must have occupied him more than it does most mortals now.

Yet revising and publishing old works, and listening to the Bible and the classics, as read to him by his friends, and playing and hearing music were not, we may be sure, the chief delight of the aged Milton. Nor was this to be found in recollections of the tremendous and perilous times through which he had passed, in reminiscences of Cromwell and other great men, or even in pardonable pride of the *quorum pars magna* kind. His chief delight, in spite of his blindness, was in his visions — his visions of empyrean glory, denied to all other men save his three compeers, Homer, Shakspere, and Dante. With such visions he lived until the end came, on November 8, 1674, having tasted the blessings of immortality while yet a mortal.

But what, in conclusion, are the main ideas about Milton the man that we should carry away, whether from reading a mere sketch like the above, or from studying Professor Masson's monumental biography, probably the most elaborate tribute ever paid to a man of letters? This question is not easy to answer, because it is never easy to speak adequately about a supreme genius; but we must attempt some sort of answer.

In the first place, we ought to remember that Milton is the great idealist of our Anglo-Saxon race. In him there was no shadow of turning from the lines of thought and action marked out for him by his presiding genius. His lines may not be our lines; but if we cannot admire to the full his ideal steadfastness of purpose and his masterful accomplishment, it is because our own capacity for the comprehension and pursuit of the ideal is in so far weak and vacillating. And it is this pure idealism of his that makes him by far the most important figure, from a moral point of view, among all Anglo-Saxons; for the genius of the race is practical, not ideal, — compromise is everywhere regarded with favor as a working principle, — and the main lesson we have all to learn is how to stand out unflinchingly for the true, the beautiful, and the good, regardless of merely present and practical considerations. We have glorified the compromising man of action at the expense of the ideal theorist until we have deluded ourselves into believing that men, who are, above all, reasoning creatures, have succeeded best when they have acted illogically, and we have thus held back reforms by contenting ourselves with halfway improvements. A due admiration for Milton's unflinching idealism, both of thought and action, will at least make it impossible for us to tolerate the charlatanism of compromise.

In the second place, we should admire Milton's consummate power of artistic accomplishment. He is the master workman of our men of letters, and this genius for perfection manifested itself in all that he undertook. In him there was no haste or waste. Whether as a youthful student at school or college, or as a scholarly recluse among his books at Horton, or as a traveller seeking culture, or as a schoolmaster, or as a political and theological controversialist, or as diplomatic secretary, or finally as a great epic poet, Milton is always found, not merely doing successfully and admirably, but doing his marvellous best. There are as few ups and downs in his work of whatever kind as are to be found in the works of any other man save perhaps Homer. He is always girded. Slowness and somewhat of sluggishness may perhaps be charged against him, but in view of his lofty conception of the need of adequate preparation, such a charge must be very tentative. He is *par excellence* the perfect conscious artist among Anglo-Saxons — as unerring as Raphael, as sublime as Michelangelo.

But he is more than idealist or artist — he was a superlatively noble, brave, truly conscientious man, who could never have intentionally done a mean thing; who was pure and clean in thought, speech, and action; who was patriotic to the point of sublime self-sacrifice; who loved his neighbor to the point of risking his life for republican principles of liberty; who, finally, spent his every moment as in the sight of the God he both worshipped and loved. Possessed of sublime powers, his thought was to make the best use of them to the glory of God and the good of his fellow-man. We may not think that he always succeeded; but who among the men of our race save Washington is such an exemplar of high and holy and effective purpose? Beside his white and splendid flame nearly all the other great spirits of earth burn yellow, if not low. Truly, as Wordsworth said, his soul was like a star; and, if it dwelt apart, should we therefore love it the less? It is more difficult to love the sublime than to love the approximately human, but the necessity for such love is the essence of the first and greatest commandment.

In conclusion, we may remember that whatever may be thought of the claims just set forth, which will not be admitted in their entirety by any one who has not made Milton an object of lifelong devotion, there are two facts that render a study of his life and works essential to all persons who would fain have the slightest claim to be considered cultured men.

The first is that Milton has unquestionably influenced his country's literature more than any other English man of letters, unless it be Shakspere. Although he did not live to reap the reward of the fame that "Paradise Lost" began to attract, even before the close of the seventeenth century, he must have felt sure that he had built himself an enduring monument. His conviction was true. Certainly, from the appearance of Addison's criticism of the great epic to the present day, no English poet of any note has failed at one time or another to pass under his spell. Even Pope borrowed from him; and Thomson, Dyer, Collins, and Gray were his open disciples. What Cowper and Wordsworth would have been without him is hard to imagine. The youthful Keats imitated him, Byron tried to rival him, and Shelley sang that "his clear sprite yet reigns o'er earth the third among the sons of light." As for Landor, Tennyson, Browning, Arnold, and Swinburne, their direct or indirect debt to him is plain to every student. With regard to his prose, which has never been sufficiently studied, the case has been somewhat different. It is the old story of the bow of Ulysses. But it cannot be doubted that if on the formal side our modern writers look back to Cowley and Dryden, and that if Burke is the only specific author in whom a critic like Lowell can discover definite traces of the influence of Milton, there has never been a master of sonorous and eloquent prose who did not owe more than he was perhaps aware of to the author of "Areopagitica."

The second fact is equally patent, but less often insisted upon. It is that in the triumphant progress of the Anglo-Saxon race, whether in the mother island, in America, or in Australia, whatever has been won for the cause of civic or religious or mental liberty has been won along lines that Milton would have approved in the main had he been living; has been won by men more or less inspired by him; and will be kept only by men who are capable of appreciating rightly the height and breadth and depth of his splendid and ineffable personality.

PART II.—WORKS

CHAPTER I

EARLIEST POEMS IN ENGLISH

In discussing Milton's minor poems, exclusive of the sonnets, it is well to adopt some convenient lines of division. There is so little that is juvenile about his work that the usual twofold classification will hardly suffice; there is such variety that his own separation into Latin and English is not fully satisfactory. Perhaps we shall do well to adopt a new division of our own—to treat first the English poems written before the retirement at Horton, excluding the elegies; next the Latin poems, except the "Epitaphium Damonis," and kindred verses; then the companion poems, "L'Allegro" and "Il Penseroso," with a few pendant pieces; then "Arcades" and "Comus," both being masques; and finally "Lycidas," together with the other elegies of which it is the crown. This division has the advantage of being sufficiently chronological, while at the same time it groups the poems according to their kinds.

We have already seen that as a boy of fifteen Milton attempted paraphrases of Psalms cxiv. and cxxxvi. It was just such a beginning as might have been expected of him, and as the pieces probably represent all that we have of his ante-Cambridge compositions, they possess considerable interest. Minute critics have inferred from them his acquaintance with Spenser and Sylvester's translation of Du Bartas, but it would be fairer to lay stress on the original vigor displayed.

> "And caused the golden-tressèd sun
> All the day long his course to run,"

and

> "The ruddy waves he cleft in twain
> Of the Erythræan main,"

are couplets premonitory of the splendid rhythm of the later works, whether or not they contain borrowed epithets.

The English poems composed at Cambridge

number exactly eleven, if the little "Song on May Morning" be assigned to that period. Five of these, the elegies on the "Fair Infant" and the Marchioness of Winchester, the two humorous pieces on Hobson, the carrier, and the lines on Shakspere, can be best discussed in detail along with "Lycidas." Two of the others are sonnets, and will be appropriately treated with their fellow-poems in this form. We are thus left to take account of only four pieces, a complete and a fragmentary ode, a song, and an academical exercise — an amount of verse that would be unworthy of separate treatment but for the fact that it contains Milton's single ode, one of the supreme specimens of its class in our literature. Before discussing it, however, we must remember that while these eleven Cambridge poems do not represent great fecundity, they do represent both scope and mastery of genius. The two serious elegies are excellent, the lines on Shakspere are noble and indicative of a fine culture, and the sonnets are marked by pure, if serious, charm. In short, it is a body of verse full of promise, as well as evidencing much achievement — an achievement sufficient, had he never written another line, to have preserved Milton's name along with those of Barnfield and other minor Elizabethans, though in a somewhat higher category.

The elegy on a "Fair Infant" seems to date from Milton's second year at Cambridge, 1625–26; next in chronological order comes the fragmentary "At a Vacation Exercise," which dates from 1628, the year before he took his Bachelor's degree. He had been appointed to deliver a Latin speech at certain sportive exercises held by the undergraduates. His thesis was the familiar one that all work and no play makes Jack a dull boy, but he presented it under a much more decorous title. He was assisted by other students who represented fictitious characters — on this special occasion the "Predicaments" of Aristotle. Milton, in spite of his serious nature, managed to play well his part of "Father" to the unruly assemblage, hence his speech contains jocularities and now unintelligible personal allusions. Suddenly he introduced an innovation; he passed from Latin into English, apostrophizing nobly his native tongue, and declaiming solemnly fifty sonorous couplets. Much of the poem is dead to us now; but the style cannot die, because it is prophetic of the future master. Even the undergraduates bent on fun must have stood dumb with pride for their brilliant colleague who could thus sing, —

> "Of kings and queens and heroes old,
> Such as the wise Demodocus once told
> In solemn songs at King Alcinous' feast."

But Milton would not try their patience, for he soon called up his "Predicaments," and ended with some lines about the chief English rivers that long puzzled the critics until it was discovered not many years ago that the dignified poet was probably punning on the names of two young freshmen, sons of a Sir John Rivers.

His next poetic performance, dating from Christmas, 1629, must have still more astonished his fellow-students, if any of them were permitted to hear it. The famous stanzas entitled "On the Morning of Christ's Nativity," which Hallam has declared to be an ode, "perhaps the finest in the English language," represent a marked growth of poetic power and an exceptional accomplishment for a poet just turned twenty-one. He thought enough of it to give an excellent description of it to his friend Diodati in his sixth Latin elegy; indeed the original hardly anywhere rises above two splendid lines of the paraphrase:—

> "Stelliparumque polum, modulantesque æthere turmas
> Et subito elisos ad sua fana deos."[1]

As we shall see from the fragment on the "Passion," Milton was meditating upon the great events of the Christian Year and endeavoring to give them poetic expression of an adequate kind. He succeeded so well at his first attempt that he may almost be said to have imposed the thought of his ode and himself upon most reading people whenever the glad festival comes round. Reverence of spirit and noble charm of style had never be-

[1] Loosely rendered by Cowper:—

> "The hymning angels and the herald-star
> That led the Wise, who sought him from afar,
> And idols on their own unhallow'd shore
> Dash'd, at his birth to be revered no more."

fore been so harmonized in an English religious poem, nor have they, perhaps, been so harmonized since. The poet was rapt away on the wings of his imagination, but not carried so far out of sight as in much of his later work; hence his ode is one of the most comprehensible of his poems for the normal reader.

Whether, indeed, it deserves Hallam's high praise is another matter. It has action, but not the dramatic intensity of Dryden's "Alexander's Feast"; it has nobility of thought and feeling, but not the nobility of the best stanzas of Wordsworth's "Ode on the Intimations of Immortality." Besides, being a regular ode in set stanzas, it did not allow Milton to attain the full harmonic effects of the more or less irregular ode, in which sound is married to sense in a manner unparalleled in any other form of lyric. Yet, if it be not the greatest English ode, it surely deserves more attention than Mark Pattison gave it, not to mention the purblind Johnson. There are crudities to be discovered in it beyond doubt; there are indications of a slight bending toward the

Fantastic School of Donne; but these are trifles compared with the charm and power that result from the blending of Greek and Hebrew elements — with the almost magical effects of the skilfully chosen proper names — with the pervading dignity of style and the individual mastery of rhythm.

With regard to the last point it will be well to go somewhat into particulars. Not only is the rhythm of such a stanza as that beginning

"Such music (as 'tis said)"

masterly and original, but the stanzaic form itself is the invention of a metrical artist. Its elements are not new, being merely a "tail-stave" and a couplet; but the proportions observed by the various lines with respect to the number of contained syllables are strikingly unique. The short lines of five or six syllables are balanced against lines of ten, and when one expects a uniform couplet, one is confronted with a line of eight syllables rhyming with an Alexandrine of twelve. Hence the resulting stanza gives swiftness of movement through its short lines, abundance of melody through its frequent rhymes, and a stately dignity through its protracted and sonorous close. What finer combination of melody and harmony could one desire than this: —

"The lonely mountains o'er,
And the resounding shore,
A voice of weeping heard and loud lament;
From haunted spring, and dale,
Edged with poplar pale,
The parting Genius is with sighing sent;
With flower-inwoven tresses torn
The Nymphs in twilight shade of tangled thickets mourn."

The alliteration discoverable here and elsewhere has induced some critics to find the ode too artificial, just as the twenty-sixth stanza about "the sun in bed," introducing a figure more suitable to Donne, or, with a slight change, to Butler, has induced them to discover a hankering in the young poet after the diseased beauties of Marinism; but these are trifles when compared with the splendid rhythmical and metrical triumph of the

"Hymn" proper, or with the marvellous diction exhibited in such verses as

> "And cast the dark foundations deep,
> And bid the weltering waves their oozy channel keep."

With regard to the four admirable preliminary stanzas, Milton can claim no such metrical originality as he can for the stanzas of his "Hymn." They are precisely the stanzas used in the elegy on the "Fair Infant," and are a mere modification of the rhyme-royal of Chaucer, the seventh verse containing twelve syllables instead of ten, *i.e.* being an Alexandrine. This modification had been consciously or unconsciously made by Sir Thomas More, in his "Lamentation" for Queen Elizabeth, wife of Henry VII., but Phineas Fletcher was more probably the source that influenced Milton. He might easily have developed it for himself, however, since modifications of stanzas by the addition of an Alexandrine in imitation of Spenser were frequent at the time. But such noble use of any sort of stanza as that made by Milton was not common then, and never has been or will be.

The Easter season of 1630 evidently found Milton preparing to emulate his success of the preceding Christmas. He began with eight introductory stanzas of the same modified rhyme-royal form; but at the end of the eighth, before he reached the "Hymn" proper, he broke off, appending to the fragment years later the following note:—

"This subject the author, finding to be above the years he had when he wrote it, and nothing satisfied with what was begun, left it unfinished."

With this judgment it is easy to agree. The stanzas, while not lacking in beauty, are not worthy of the transcendent subject. They show more markedly than his preceding poems the influence of his favorite Spenser, and they do not show to the full the splendid original powers of which Milton had already given such evidence. They mark also the limit of his yielding to the fantastic absurdities of Marinism, for there is little in the poetry of Quarles or Sylvester that is more extravagant than the monumental "conceit," in the seventh stanza, of "that sad sepulchral rock," upon whose "softened quarry" the poet "would score" his "plaining verse as lively as before."

If the little "Song on May Morning" dates from 1630, it more than atones by its beauty for the failure of the poem on the "Passion." But, as we shall see later, there is a tendency among critics to assign the undated early poems to the period of retirement at Horton; hence the ten beautiful lines may not represent the emotions of the college student at all. They are full of an exquisite feeling for spring, especially for its pulsing energy, which is well symbolized by the sudden change at the fifth verse from long iambic lines to shorter trochaic ones. Why a student like Milton, who had celebrated the return of spring in Latin elegiacs, might not have written this song after a walk in the beautiful gardens of Trinity is hard to see; but the critics seem to write as if Milton's love of nature was brought out at Horton alone. Of this we shall speak hereafter; it is sufficient now to emphasize the beauty of the lines, which is more elaborate, however, than befits a genuine song.

CHAPTER II

THE LATIN POEMS

As we have seen, the Latin poems formed a separate portion of the volume of 1645-46. They filled eighty-eight pages, divided by their author into two books, one of elegies ("Elegiarum Liber"), and one of miscellanies ("Sylvarum Liber"). In the poem last written, the "Epitaphium Damonis," Milton announced his intention of writing thenceforward in English, a promise which was practically kept, since nothing but the "Ode to Rous" and a few epigrams were subsequently added to the collection. Of the seven elegies, eight epigrams, and nine miscellaneous pieces (excluding the three Greek poems) printed in 1645, twelve were written at Cambridge, one apparently at Horton, and the rest during or shortly after the Italian journey. The whole is therefore the work of a young man, and a considerable portion that of a mere youth. Judged from this point of view, it is a wonderful achievement.

With regard to the intrinsic merits of the verses, there is almost complete unanimity among the most qualified critics. With the exception of Landor, who wrote more as a Roman, to whom Latin seemed, in the words of Dr. Garnett, to come "like the language of some prior state of existence, rather remembered than learned," Milton is the greatest English writer of Latin verse. This may seem to be a dubious compliment in an age when even the veritable classics are often disparaged; but it would not have been such to Milton and his contemporaries, and it must mean something in any careful estimate of his work. He is the greater man and poet for having succeeded so well in his Latin verses, even if we believe with Dr. Garnett that he won his success by the sweat of his brow—a point that does not seem to be irrevocably settled.

Authorities are agreed that Milton always attained scholarly elegance, and that he did not lose his own individuality as is so often the case with writers who attempt to use a language not native to them. That he succeeded in writing great poems is hardly asserted, save with regard to the "Epitaphium Damonis," of the nobility and beauty of which there has been no serious doubt. Difference of opinion has revealed itself as to what author Milton followed most closely, Warton, a good judge, believing that he imitated Ovid with consistency, Hallam maintaining that his hexameters at least are more Virgilian. It is safer, perhaps, to side with Warton. It is safe, too, to agree with Dr. Johnson and with Dr. Garnett that, in the words of the former, neither "power of invention" nor "vigor of sentiment" are so conspicuous as "the purity of the diction and the harmony of the numbers"; but on this point something needs to be said by way of explanation.

Milton's diction is pure on the whole, but it is easy to establish the fact that he uses quite a number of ante- and post-classical words; more, seemingly, of the former than of the latter. His excessive and sometimes inaccurate use of "que" is also to be noticed![1] Harmonious his verses certainly are when he is using the elegiac couplet; but it may be questioned whether vigor is not rather the chief characteristic of his hexameters. Again, it is a mistake to suppose that there are no remarkably poetic passages to be found outside the "Epitaphium Damonis" and the two elegies (i., vi.) to Diodati, as might be inferred from the prominence given these poems. Such are to be found even outside the lines "Ad Patrem" and the tribute to Manso, which some modern critics praise. The close of the fourth elegy to Thomas Young, Milton's tutor, is full of sonorous energy; there is a fine lift in the early verses on the "Return of Spring"; and there is probably more sheer dramatic power in the

[1] In an interesting letter my friend Professor Charles W. Bain of South Carolina College informs me that Ovid seems to have had a preponderant influence on Milton's diction, also that the latter uses an excess of purely poetic words as well as quite a number rendered classical only by a single use on the part of Ovid or Virgil. Mr. Bain thinks Milton's versification remarkably good, but his trained ear supports my untrained one in finding not a few verses rendered unpleasant by a superfluity of elided syllables.

strong hexameters on Guy Fawkes's Day ("In Quintum Novembris"), written when Milton was not quite eighteen, than is to be found in the rest of his Latin verse, or indeed in the poetry of any other poet of equal age. There is strong work, too, in both the academical exercises included in the "Sylvarum Liber." In short, while the Milton of the Latin poems is plainly more graceful than sublime, he is just as plainly a Milton destined to grow greater with the years.

There is little need in a study like the present to dwell at length on special poems. The elegies on the Bishops of Ely and Winchester, on the Cambridge beadle and vice-chancellor, and on Diodati will occupy us in a later chapter. None of the epigrams can be called great, or even fine, although some are good; and the irregular ode to John Rous, the librarian at Oxford, who had lost his copy of the edition of the "Minor Poems" of 1645 and desired another, is interesting chiefly as a metrical experiment. The two Greek epigrams and the paraphrase of Psalm cxiv. are not remarkable, and the scazons to the ailing Roman, Giovanni

Salzilli, who had praised Milton so extravagantly, are little more than graceful. But the elegies to Diodati — really friendly letters in verse — are excellent of their kind, the later written being notable for its fine expression of that cardinal doctrine of Milton's faith, afterward so nobly presented in "Comus" and in a memorable prose passage, — that he who would write a true poem must live a pure life. The elegy or letter to Young is full of reverent affection, and the lines on the advent of spring have a distinct charm. The seventh elegy is interesting from its somewhat conventional but graphic description of the effect upon the young poet of a pretty face flashing upon him in a London street, but immediately disappearing in the crowd. Later, Milton appended some lines of apology for his youthful enthusiasm, but they were not needed; the occurrence described was evidently a rare one.

The "Sylvarum Liber" adds more to Milton's fame than the technical elegies do. The "In Quintum Novembris" is, as we have seen, a memorable poem, even if it ends flatly. The description of Satan arousing the Pope to send his emissaries to England is very vivid, and ought to be read in Professor Masson's hexameters, since the gentle Cowper was too squeamish to translate it, and the high-church Johnson to praise it. The academical exercises, especially that on Aristotle's view of Plato's philosophy, show how Milton could clothe with life even the dry bones of metaphysics, just as he afterward clothed those of theology. The lines to his father are not only a fine filial tribute, but are a splendid autobiographical defence of the right of genius to careful culture and to exemption from all sordid incentives to self-exertion. It is as noble a document as can be found in the annals of human intercourse, and should be studied by all who know Latin. Almost as much can be said of the "Mansus," the admirable tribute to that Marquis Manso who has the unique distinction, denied even to Mæcenas, of being the friend of two great epic poets of different tongues, Tasso and Milton. The aged Neapolitan has his name enshrined in Tasso's verses, but he has as sure a title to fame in Milton's tribute. The English reader may indeed bear away from the poem a deep regret that Milton never carried out his expressed purpose of writing an epic on King Arthur, but he will always remember with pleasure the hale and hearty friend of genius—the *Diis dilecte senex*. He will pass on, too, to read the beautiful description of Manso's goblets in the "Epitaphium Damonis," and having finished the two noble poems, he will ever after find it impossible to speak of Milton's Latin verses without affection mixed with wonder.

CHAPTER III

"L'ALLEGRO" AND "IL PENSEROSO"

THE genesis of "L'Allegro" and "Il Penseroso," perhaps the best known and most heartily admired of all Milton's compositions, is involved in considerable obscurity. They were not printed before 1645, and they do not exist for us in the celebrated bound volume of Milton's Mss. in the library of Trinity College, Cambridge, which contains the drafts of all the English poems written between 1633, probably, and 1645; we are therefore compelled, in the absence of other data, to rely upon inferences and internal evidence in determining their time and place of writing. The consensus of critical opinion gives 1632–33 as the time, and Horton as the place. Professor Masson assigns them to the latter half of 1632. There are, however, reasons to make one think that they should probably be placed earlier. The autumn of 1632 seems to be selected because Horton is usually assumed as the place of composition, and Milton went to reside there in July, 1632. He would naturally, argue the critics, be so impressed with the charms of the spot that he would turn to verse, and "L'Allegro" and "Il Penseroso," and the "Song on May Morning," which we have assigned to the Cambridge period, would be the outcome. But there is no proof that the poems were not written at Cambridge or in London as reminiscential tributes to the pleasures of a vacation spent in the country; and we know from a Latin prolusion or oration delivered, Masson thinks, either in the latter half of 1631 or the first part of 1632, that Milton spent "the last past summer . . . . amid rural scenes and sequestered glades," and that he recalled "the supreme delight *he* had with the Muses." This vacation of 1631 may have been spent at Horton, for there is no proof that the elder Milton had not then acquired that property, and the young poet may have written his poems under the elms that so fascinated him, or have composed them on his return to college.

I incline to the former supposition. As we shall see, he was unquestionably supplied with hints for both his poems by Burton's "Anatomy," surely a likely book for such a student as Milton to take with him on a vacation. Again, no one can read the "Prolusion on Early Rising," almost certainly Milton's, without thinking that much of the raw material of the two poems was in his brain and being expressed during his university life; nor can one read the other prolusions without seeing that Orpheus, the music of the spheres, and Platonism were much in his thoughts. Besides, about 1630, the date of the "Epitaph on Shakspere," Milton was evidently to some extent occupied with his great forerunner, whose genius is honored in the poems, and a year later he was experimenting with the octosyllabic couplet in the "Epitaph on the Marchioness of Winchester." Finally, it was about this time that he was seriously weighing the reasons *pro* and *con* with regard to his choice of a profession, and it might naturally occur to him to contrast in poetic form the pleasures of the more or less worldly and the more or less secluded, studious, and devoted life. He had made his choice by the autumn of 1632, and had therefore less cause for such poetical expression.

A minute analysis of the style and metre of the poems tends to confirm the view expressed above. It is obviously a transitional style when compared with that of the "Nativity Ode," and other earlier pieces. Scriptural ideas and subjects are occupying his mind less, and he has progressed toward a freer handling of his themes. He has become interested in contemporary English poetry, and while showing the influence of the classics, is not mastered by them. All this would indicate that the poems were written after 1631, though, as we have just seen, it is not unlikely that having in that year handled the octosyllabic couplet successfully, he should shortly be tempted to try it again. We thus have 1631 as a *terminus a quo;* 1633–1634, the years of "Arcades" and "Comus," are a *terminus ad quem* for the following strictly metrical reasons. The lyrical portions of "Arcades" and "Comus" appear to be less spontaneous and more mature than "L'Allegro" and its companion poem. The metrical art displayed is more elaborate and self-conscious, and when one looks closer, as, for example, when one compares the invocation to Mirth in "L'Allegro" with the similar passage in "Comus" (ll. 102–122), one is struck with the fact that the verses of the anti-masque have lost the blithe sensuousness of the former poem, that thought is struggling with feeling, and that the lyric style of the poet is approaching its culmination in the elaborate and highly sustained art that has made "Lycidas" matchless. We conclude, therefore, that "L'Allegro" and "Il Penseroso" are nearer to the "Epitaph on the Marchioness of Winchester" than they are to "Arcades"; and if any one should argue that the mature sentiment of the poems and their vigorous expression indicate a later, not an earlier, date, it must suffice to reply that youth takes itself more seriously than age, and that there is no sentiment or thought in either poem that Milton might not well have had as a student at Cambridge.

It has been stated already that Milton was

indebted for hints, if not for direct suggestion, to Burton's "Anatomy of Melancholy." This famous book, the first edition of which appeared in 1621, was prefaced by a poem entitled "The Author's Abstract of Melancholy, Διαλογῶς," in which "Democritus Junior" analyzes his feelings in a way that foreshadows Milton's subsequent procedure. There are twelve stanzas of eight lines each, the last two verses of each stanza constituting a variable refrain, the measure being, however, the octosyllabic couplet. In one stanza the pleasures of a meditative man are given in a series of little pictures, while the next stanza presents the woes of the same personage when a fit of real melancholy is upon him. Milton could not have failed to be struck with the general effectiveness of the idea and its development, but his artist's instinct told him that this effectiveness would be enhanced if, instead of a dialogue in stanzas, he should write two distinct but companion poems, developed on parallel lines, in which the pleasures of a typically cheerful and a typically serious man should be described in pictures slightly more elaborate than those of Burton. He abandoned the too glaring contrast of joys and woes, and succeeded also in avoiding the occasional dropping into commonplace that mars the "Abstract of Melancholy." But some pictures and even lines and phrases of the elder poem probably remained in his memory.

Another poem which may have influenced Milton is the song, "Hence, all you vain delights," in Fletcher's play, "The Nice Valour." This play was not published until 1647, but it had been acted long before, and the song had almost certainly become known before "Il Penseroso" was written. Tradition assigns the lyric to Beaumont, but Mr. Bullen with more probability gives it to Fletcher. It is an exquisite expansion of the theme expressed in its closing verse, "Nothing's so dainty-sweet as lovely melancholy," and it is pleasant to believe that it may have given Milton a hint, although it can scarcely have had as much influence upon his verses as his own two poems plainly had upon a stanza of Collins's "The Passions." There are naturally traces of other poets to be found in these productions of Milton's impressionable period, particularly of Joshua Sylvester, and to a less degree of Spenser, Browne, and Marlowe. Collins, too, was not the only eighteenth-century poet who had "L'Allegro" and "Il Penseroso" ringing through his head, as any one may see who will take the trouble to examine Dodsley's well-known collection. Even Pope was not above borrowing epithets from them, and Dyer's best poem, "Grongar Hill," would not have had its being without them. Matthew Green, Thomas Warton, John Hughes, who actually wrote a new conclusion for "Il Penseroso," and other minor verse-writers were much affected by them, and Gray borrowed from them with the open boldness that always marks the appropriations of a true poet. But perhaps the best proof of their popularity during a century which is too sweepingly charged with inability to appreciate real poetry, is the fact that Handel set them to music. In our own century they have never lacked admirers, or failed to exert upon poets an easily detected influence. It may even be held with some show of reason that their popularity, leading to a fuller knowledge of Milton, paved the way for the remarkable renascence of Spenser in the latter half of the eighteenth and the first part of the present century.

As their Italian titles imply, the subjects or speakers of Milton's verses are The Cheerful Man and The Thoughtful (Meditative) Man respectively. Our English adjectives do not quite adequately render the Italian they are intended to translate, which is perhaps the reason why Milton went abroad for his titles, since he had a striking warning before him in Burton's "Abstract" of the ambiguity attaching to such a word as "melancholy," which he might have used with one of his poems without exciting surprise. He has excited surprise with some modern critics through the fact that he wrote *Penseroso* instead of *Pensieroso*, but it has been seemingly shown that the form he used was correct and current when he wrote. His Italian titles, however, have not prevented much discussion as to the characters he intended to portray. Critics are quite unanimously of the opinion that Il

Penseroso represents a man very like the Milton we know, but they are divided as to the kind of man typified by L'Allegro. One editor, Mr. Verity, goes so far as to say that Milton "must have felt that the character of L'Allegro might, with slight changes or additions, be made to typify the careless, pleasure-seeking spirit of the Cavaliers and Court; the spirit which he afterward figured in Comus and his followers, and condemned to destruction." If this view be correct, one is forced to conclude that Milton had more of the true dramatist's power of creating characters other than himself than he has generally been supposed to possess; and it requires us to conceive the more sprightly poem as forming a hard mechanical contrast to its companion, which is the reverse of poetical. On the other hand, Dr. Garnett maintains that the two poems "are complementary rather than contrary, and may be, in a sense, regarded as one poem, whose theme is the praise of the reasonable life." It is easy to agree with this view, especially as Burton's poem obviously suggested the idea of contrasting two well-marked moods of one individual character, rather than that of bringing into juxtaposition two radically different characters. L'Allegro may not be the Milton who meditated entering the Church and making his life a true poem, but he is rather the Milton who went to the theatre in his youth, and could in his mature age ask Lawrence

> "What neat repast shall feast us, light and choice,
> Of Attic taste with wine, whence we may rise
> To hear the lute well touched or artful voice
> Warble immortal notes and Tuscan air?"

than the typical Cavalier of Charles's court. Cavaliers did not usually call for "sweet Liberty" but for sweet License, nor did they greatly hanker after "unreprovèd pleasures." They were not particularly noted for their early rising; and if any one of them had watched the Bear out, in different pursuits from those of Il Penseroso, he would probably not have continued his morning walk after encountering the "milk maid singing blithe."

Another point on which critics differ is, whether or not Milton intended to describe the events of a day of twenty-four hours.

Some claim that he merely sketches the general tenor of the life of his characters; others that he represents the events of an ideal day. The antagonists ought to be satisfied with the assurance that he intended to do both the one thing and the other. The careful and sequential division of the day that is apparent in each poem (even if "Il Penseroso" does begin with the nightingale and the moon) cannot be accidental, nor can the grouping of events and natural sights belonging to different seasons of the year be the result of ignorance or negligence.

It is, probably, a fad of criticism to call as much attention as is now done to the fact that Milton was not so accurate or so penetrating an observer of nature as some of his successors, like Tennyson, have been. In the first place, neither here nor in "Paradise Lost" will Milton be found to be much of a sinner in this regard if he be compared with his predecessors and contemporaries. In the second place, it is by no means certain that minute and accurate observation of nature is essential to the equipment of a great poet. A genuine love of nature, a power to feel and impart something of her spirit, is doubtless essential; but as poetry on its pictorial side should be mainly suggestive, it is not yet clear that posterity will get more pleasure out of the elaborate and accurate pictures of some modern poets than out of the broadly true and suggestive, if sometimes inaccurate, pictures of Milton. It is not entirely unlikely that our recently developed love of detail-work has injured our sense for form, and that our grandchildren will take Matthew Arnold's advice and return to the Greeks — and Milton, in order to learn what the highest poetry really is like. Milton is nearer akin to Homer and Sophocles than he is to the modern naturalist or nature mystic, and it is well for English poetry that he is. He would probably have thought the picture of the sunbeams lying in the golden chamber, suggested by a few words in that exquisite fragment of Mimnermus beginning "Αἰήταο πόλιν," more in keeping with the requirements of a rational poetics than nine-tenths of the purple descriptive passages in English poetry since the days of Wordsworth.

Yet if editors and critics have had their

humors and fads, they have always ended by acknowledging the perennial charm of these poems. And the mass of readers has paid its highest tribute of culling many a phrase and verse for quotation to please the outer or the inner ear. The anthologist of our lyric poetry who should omit them from his collection would pay dearly for his indiscretion, and yet he could argue fairly that they are rather idylls than true lyrics, as Wordsworth did long since. But if they are, in fact, a series of little pictures, sometimes so loosely joined or so hastily sketched as to puzzle the careful critic,[1] these have been so fused into one organic whole by the delicate, evanescent sentiment that pervades each poem that even the purist will be willing to admit them to be lyrics of marvellous beauty and power, coming from the heart of the poet and going straight to the hearts of his readers.

With Milton's most popular poems it is convenient to group three short pieces that are little known. They are those entitled "At a

[1] There are three or four passages in the poems rendered very obscure by a looseness of syntax unusual with Milton. See "L'Allegro," ll. 45–48, 103–106, and "Il Penseroso," ll. 147–150.

Solemn Music," "On Time," and "Upon the Circumcision." The end of 1633 and the beginning of 1634 may be assigned as the probable period of composition, for reasons that need not be detailed here. The first poem seems reminiscential of a sacred concert, the second was intended as an inscription for a clock-face, the third forms, with the "Nativity Ode" and the stanzas on "The Passion," a somewhat belated member of a religious trilogy. All three pieces are very elaborate in style and are nearer to "Arcades," "Comus," and "Lycidas" than to "L'Allegro" and "Il Penseroso." All are full of high solemnity and of that mighty vision of eternal things that makes "Paradise Lost" so supreme in the world's poetry. The following lines from the first will illustrate the quality of the trio better than any description: —

"Where the bright Seraphim in burning row
Their loud uplifted angel-trumpets blow,
And the Cherubic host in thousand quires
Touch their immortal harps of golden wires
With those just spirits that wear victorious palms,
Hymns devout and holy songs
Singing everlastingly."

Such poetry ought to be better known for its intrinsic merits, but students of Milton should examine each of the poems carefully on account of the light it throws on the progress of Milton's metrical art. As Professor Masson has observed, they are proof that the poet was at this time engaged in making metrical experiments. The first two are a mixture of couplets and quatrains with one displaced rhyme; the last consists of two fourteen-lined stanzas that correspond with one another, but are exceedingly irregular in their internal structure. The most important point, however, is that in all three there is a combination of short and long lines that points forward to "Lycidas," and proves that Milton was varying the metrical experiments he had been making from his earliest youth. As late as "L'Allegro" and "Il Penseroso," in which he had experimented with a combination of trimeters and pentameters as a fitting proem for the lighter octosyllabics that were to follow, his experiments were mainly, if not entirely, along English lines; after his residence at Horton had increased his reading of the Italian poets, his verse began to show their influence, except in "Comus" and "Arcades," for which he had better models nearer home, although even in the former it may be perhaps detected. This is, of course, quite a technical matter, but it throws light upon Milton's bold yet painstaking character as an artist, and it may be used as a partial test in determining the dates of his unassigned compositions.

CHAPTER IV

"ARCADES" AND "COMUS"

MILTON had had some little experience in writing masques before he reached in "Comus" the supreme success possible in this form of composition, and he must have seen and read not a few. Although we cannot determine the exact date of "Arcades," it is reasonably certain that it preceded "Comus," and that it may be assigned to 1633. It formed only "part of an entertainment presented to the Countess Dowager of Derby at Harefield," but we may be sure that it was a part as important as it was beautiful, and that the poet's 'prentice hand was strengthened by writing it. He seems to have been induced thus to honor a lady whose praises Spenser had previously sung by the well-known musician, Henry Lawes, to whom he afterward dedicated a fine sonnet. Lawes (1595–1662) was the chief English composer of his time, and must have known the Milton family for some years. His talents won him a position at court, and the friendship of the leading poets of the time, whose songs he set to music, receiving in return their poetical encomiums. He probably gained more money, however, by furnishing music for the then fashionable masques, so we find him collaborating in the performance of Shirley's "Triumph of Peace," and composing single-handed the music of Carew's "Cœlum Britannicum." He was also music tutor to the children of the Earl and Countess of Bridgewater, which seems to explain his assumed connection with "Arcades." These children would take part in the proposed entertainment to their grandmother, and would ask their instructor's help. He, knowing Milton well, would apply to him for the necessary verses, rather than to professional masque-writers, who would probably not care to undertake such a slight piece of work. Milton's success was so conspicuous that when another and more elaborate entertainment was contemplated by the Bridgewater family, Lawes would again apply to him for poetical assistance. This is a simple, if meagre, account of the way the young Puritan poet was enlisted in the service of the distinguished Cavalier family, for Warton's statement that Milton's father was the Earl's tenant at Horton has not been substantiated.

With regard to the poetical merits of "Arcades" there can scarcely be two opinions. The speech of the Genius of the Wood, in heroic couplets, is a triumph of style, and the three songs have a lightness of touch that is rare in Milton's lyric work. The compliments that had to be paid the Dowager are turned with as much grace as if the Puritan had been an Elizabethan of the prime. Indeed Shakspere himself has hardly surpassed the exquisite song beginning

"O'er the smooth enamelled green,"

while he surely would have praised, though he need not have envied, such a divinely harmonious passage as the following:—

"But else in deep of night, when drowsiness
Hath locked up mortal sense, then listen I

> To the celestial Sirens' harmony,
> That sit upon the nine infolded spheres,
> And sing to those that hold the vital shears,
> And turn the adamantine spindle round
> On which the fate of Gods and men is wound."

The occasion of the more elaborate celebration that led to the creation of "Comus" was the formal entrance of the Earl of Bridgewater upon his duties as Lord President of Wales in the autumn of 1634, at his official residence, Ludlow Castle, in Shropshire. Here there was quite a gathering of relatives and friends who would naturally think a masque to be peculiarly suitable to such a semi-royal function, especially as the three eldest children of the Earl, Lord Brackley, Mr. Thomas Egerton, and Lady Alice Egerton, had already acted in similar shows. The great hall of the castle would also be a most fitting place for the performance, and here it probably came off, on Michaelmas night (September 29), 1634.

In order to give time for the setting of the songs to music and the training of the performers, Milton must have been ready with his manuscript at least by the beginning of the summer. Lawes probably gave him such personal details about the actors and the scene of the intended performance as would enable him to insert the proper compliments and to introduce Sabrina in honor of the river Severn. It may possibly be that Milton, like the majority of his countrymen, felt that Prynne had gone too far in his "Histriomastix," and that the young Puritan was not sorry to have an opportunity to show that religious sincerity has no necessary connection with a long face. He may, too, have been glad of an occasion to measure his strength with the greatest poets of the day; and, perhaps, he may have desired to air his philosophy. But this is all mere conjecture. What we know for certain is that Lord Brackley performed the part of the First Brother, Mr. Thomas Egerton of the Second Brother, Lady Alice Egerton of the Lady, and Lawes of the Attendant Spirit. We do not know who took the part of Comus, or who composed his rout and the company of dancing shepherds,[1] but in

[1] In the normal anti-masque the performers were hired actors.

all probability other children of the Earl and his friends or retainers filled the remaining parts. We are not even informed how the masque was received, or whether Milton saw it produced; but we know that Lawes's friends asked for copies, and that to save himself trouble he had an edition published in 1637—probably from the acting copy. The name of the writer was omitted, the motto prefixed showing that his consent to publish had been given reluctantly. Neither in this nor in the editions of 1645 and 1673 was the title "Comus" employed, Milton preferring the simple designation—"A Mask." Lawes's edition was prefaced by a very complimentary letter "to the author" from the famous Provost of Eton, Sir Henry Wotton, which shows clearly what judicious critics must have thought of Milton and his work long before he became famous. In the edition of 1673 there was no need of such commendation, and the letter was omitted. It remains to add that "Comus" exists in Milton's handwriting among the Cambridge Mss., and that another copy, known as the Bridgewater Ms., is extant, which is supposed to be the acting copy, in Lawes's handwriting. The textual variations are not specially important.

But we have dwelt sufficiently upon the external features of "Comus," and must now compare it with other productions of its kind. To do this thoroughly would require a somewhat detailed account of the development of the masque from its origin, as a spectacular feature of an Italian wedding feast, to its culmination in the entertainment which Ben Jonson, Inigo Jones, Ferrabosco, Thomas Giles, and the lords and ladies of the court labored to make worthy of the favor of their pedant king, James I.—an entertainment which gave scope to the amateur actor, the engineer, the painter, the sculptor, the architect, the musician, the poet—to say nothing of the dancing-master, the dressmaker, and the upholsterer. For such a sketch we have no space here, nor can we give an analysis of a typical masque with which the reader might compare "Comus," and thus judge of the deviations of the latter from the normal form.[1] We must therefore content

[1] The reader who is interested may find good accounts of the development of the masque in Ward's "History of English

ourselves with the statement that even in such an elaborate piece as William Browne's "Inner Temple Masque," which contains some delightful poetry, the chief emphasis was laid on the scenery, the costumes, the dancing, and the music, while in "Comus," on the other hand, Milton laid as little stress as possible upon externals, and concentrated his energy chiefly on the literary side of his work. Against Browne's 329 rhyming verses he gave 1023 lines, a large portion of which belonged to the metrical form appropriate to the regular drama rather than to the masque—to wit, blank verse. These variations have led, as we shall now see, to much confusion among the critics as to the real nature of "Comus."

There are, indeed, few poems in literature with regard to which critical opinion has been more hopelessly mixed, certainly on points of detail. Some time since much amusement was caused by the statement, afterward contra-

Dramatic Literature," Symonds's "Shakspere's Predecessors in the English Drama," and Masson's "Life of Milton," vol. i. Masson analyzes Shirley's "Triumph of Peace," and I give an analysis of Browne's "Inner Temple Masque" in my edition of the "L'Allegro," etc.

dicted, that a professor in a leading university had said to his class that for his own part he did not think "Comus" was "in it" compared with "The Faithful Shepherdess." One immediately set against this jaunty dictum Macaulay's well-known opinion that Milton's great masque — "the noblest performance of the kind which exists in any language" — "is as far superior to 'The Faithful Shepherdess' as 'The Faithful Shepherdess' is to the 'Aminta,' or the 'Aminta' to the 'Pastor Fido';" and those persons who had read the four pastoral dramas named felt that for once at least in his life Macaulay shone as a critic in comparison with some of his successors. Certainly the hypothetical modern critic went far beyond even the censorious Dr. Johnson, and his extravagance confirms the need of an inquiry into the reasons for the divergence of critical opinions on the subject of "Comus."

We must remember at the outset that most of the critics, sooner or later, save themselves from ridicule by acknowledging the greatness of "Comus" as a whole. Even Dr. Johnson, after affirming that the songs contained in the masque were "harsh in their diction and not very musical in their numbers," was moved to say that "a work more truly poetical is rarely found." When a critic who was radically incapacitated for appreciating much that was best in Milton could say this of "Comus," it ought not to surprise us to find another Tory critic, Mr. Saintsbury, who can appreciate Milton, going astray in the opposite direction, and declaring that it is in "Comus" that "Milton's poetical power is at its greatest height." "Comus" is so good in parts that it is no wonder that Dr. Johnson forgot for a moment to be censorious, and Mr. Saintsbury to be entirely *bizarre*. But we are not warranted in judging a poem from the political and ecclesiastical views of its author, as Johnson practically did; or from the supreme beauty of certain of its passages, as Mr. Saintsbury seems to do. A poem must be judged as a whole, and it is just here that the critics have been most likely to go astray with regard to "Comus."

Some have insisted upon viewing it as a lyrical drama; others as an epic drama (whatever that may be); some have called it a philosophical poem; others have been pleased to dwell upon its allegorical and satirical content. Milton, however, called it a masque; and as a masque it must be judged, not as a regular drama, or as a poem, strictly so called. If now we compare "Comus" with the masques of Ben Jonson, Fletcher, Browne, and others, we shall agree with those critics who maintain that Milton has surpassed his competitors almost as completely as Shakspere has surpassed his rivals in the regular drama. "Comus" is by far the greatest English masque. But the masque, even in Milton's hands, is not the high and perfect work of art that the regular drama is in Shakspere's. It could not be, for it was a hybrid form of art, and had the defects of its qualities.

What Milton did was to take a species of courtly entertainment, of which, as we have seen, dancing, music, painting, architecture, and poetry were component parts, and eliminate, as far as he could, all of its elements save poetry. But he was compelled to retain enough of the discredited elements to keep his audience in a good humor, and to preserve the character of his composition when it should be published. The unity of a true work of art was thus unattainable from the first; and there was a dangerous pitfall before him at which he was sure to stumble. In elaborating his plot and individualizing his characters more than was customary with his predecessors in masque-writing, and especially in making considerable use of a verse form characteristic rather of the regular drama than of the masque, he was making demands upon the interest and attention of his audience (to a less extent of his readers) that could not reasonably be responded to unless he should be able to impart to his masque more of dramatic action than even Jonson had been wont to introduce into the productions of which he was so proud. With less music, scenery, and dancing, there must be more action, or the characters would merely seem to be making long speeches. But, unfortunately, Milton was not a dramatic poet. He belonged to what Mr. Theodore Watts-Dunton has happily denominated the class of poets "of relative dramatic vision"—that is, poets who, unlike the true dramatist, cannot create characters that act and speak as flesh and blood individuals, different from their creator and from one another. The personality of these quasi-dramatists is always present in their characters, who seem like puppets speaking their creators' thoughts. When the quasi-dramatist is great, the puppet will, of course, be splendid; but nothing comparable to a living, breathing Priam, or Othello, or even a Wife of Bath. When now the quasi-dramatist becomes an epic poet, like Dante in "The Divine Comedy," or Milton in "Paradise Lost," and tells about his characters, the effect is so magnificent that it is only when we compare his work with the truly dramatic epics of Homer that we can see his limitations. But when he casts his work into more or less dramatic form, when his characters no longer have him to tell about them, but must act for themselves, their puppet nature becomes only too apparent. So it is that in "Comus" Milton is compelled, by the nature of his experiment upon the masque, to give us characters in action in order to keep up our interest, and yet by the very nature of his genius must content himself with offering us noble puppets speaking his own lofty sentiments in language fit for a god, but no more capable of acting their parts like men and women than a troupe of marionettes.

This is what Dr. Johnson saw when he faulted "Comus" as a drama. But, say the critics with a charming unanimity, "Comus" is a masque and must be judged as a masque; therefore Dr. Johnson has blundered again with regard to Milton — let him be anathema! Precisely so. "Comus" must be judged as a masque, but this is just what the critics fail to do. If they would really compare "Comus" with other masques, and stop abusing Dr. Johnson, they would see that it is because Milton ignored the canons of masque-writing that he produced a work of art still more hybrid than a masque — a something between a masque and a drama which demanded for its complete success dramatic qualities that its author could not give it. If this be a correct statement of the facts in the case, it is no wonder that critics have not known just what to say about "Comus" as a whole, or that such an admirer of Milton as Dr. Garnett can find it in his heart to call the Elder Brother a prig. But what are we to say of Mr. Saintsbury's extravagant statement that the author of "Paradise Lost" reaches in "Comus" his greatest height of poetical power? It is almost as *bizarre* as Mr. Pater's desire to see the Athens of Pisistratus rather than the Athens of Pericles.

Yet how are we to explain this anomaly, that a masque which is not a true masque surpasses all other masques, and has won for its author the plaudits of nearly every cultivated reader from Sir Henry Wotton's time to our own? The answer is simple—there is no masque that so impresses us by the nobility and beauty of its conception or execution. This nobility and beauty are so conspicuous in "Comus" as to outweigh all technical defects; besides, we are now compelled to judge masques in our closets, and are therefore prone to judge them merely by the poetry they contain. Perhaps, if we could have seen one of Ben Jonson's best masques presented at court with all its superb accessories, we might not have been thoroughly disposed to acknowledge the supremacy of "Comus" as a fashionable entertainment. But if we had possessed true poetic discernment, Hallam's often-quoted remark would have applied to us — that only one performance of "Comus" ought to have been sufficient "to convince any one of taste and feeling that a great poet had arisen in England, and one partly formed in a different school from his contemporaries."

Yes, a truly great poet, differing from his predecessors and contemporaries, had arisen in England. Spenser had sung the praises of purity, but never with the masculine vigor and grace of Milton. Fletcher had employed his exquisite lyrical genius on the same theme, but had not struck Milton's clear seraphic note. Shakspere had, indeed, embodied perfect purity in Ferdinand and Miranda, but he had set them apart in an enchanted world. It remained for Milton, while he was compelled to use a similarly remote setting, to press home to us, with all the superb resources of "divine philosophy" and equally divine art, the splendid truth that purity of mind and soul and body is to be aimed at and attained in our daily life below. "Comus" may be a hybrid form of a hybrid species of composition; but it is none the less a supreme masterpiece, because it is the noblest tribute to virtue ever paid in verse.

In view of this fact many of the comments that have been made upon "Comus" by editors and critics seem to be trivial and impertinent. It matters little to any one save Milton's biographer, whether in this passage or that the poet was satirizing the court or otherwise showing his puritanical proclivities. It is always more or less interesting, however, to trace a poet's indebtedness to his predecessors, and we may therefore bring this chapter to a close by briefly discussing this point.

The often-repeated story that the masque was founded on an actual adventure that befell the Lady Alice Egerton and her brothers seems to rest on slight foundations, and is rather based on "Comus" than "Comus" on it. Putting this aside, the main sources about which critics are pretty well agreed are George Peele's play, "The Old Wives' Tale," Fletcher's "The Faithful Shepherdess," the Circe myth as detailed in the classical authors and in Spenser and his school of poets, and finally, the "Comus" of Puteanus and Jonson's masque, "Pleasure Reconciled to Virtue."

With regard to Peele's play, which was printed in 1595, there can be little doubt that it stimulated Milton's imagination, and gave him the actual kernel of his plot. As to Fletcher's delightful pastoral comedy, of which at least three editions seem to have been published before "Comus" was acted, and which had been revived as a court-play in the winter of 1633–34, it is certain that Milton was more indebted to it than Fletcher was to Tasso and Guarini. The *motif* of the two poems is the same, the power of chastity to ward off evils, yet here Milton is much more plainly lord of his native province than Fletcher is. But the effect of Fletcher's exquisite lyrical style as seen in the latter portion of "Comus" is what most closely connects the two poets. It is impossible here to bring out this influence clearly, but the reader may be confidently referred to the elder poet's work to discover the extent and quality of the younger poet's indebtedness. Our author's literary obligations with regard to his use of the Circe myth are not very definitely traceable. He naturally had recourse to the "Odyssey," directly or indirectly, for that great poem is the fountain-head of romance. Ovid had previously drawn from the same source with regard to the same subject ("Metamorphoses," lib. xiv.), and minute critics have detected in "Comus" the influence of the Roman poet. Still more patent, however, is the influence of Spenser and the great romantic poets of Italy, who sang "of forests and enchantments drear." The Circe myth is also the subject of Browne's "Inner Temple Masque," and there are several touches in "Comus" that may possibly be traceable to this rival poem.[1]

[1] Milton was too young to have seen the masque performed, and I do not find any evidence in the latest edition of Browne's poems that his charming trifle was revived; still, more than one manuscript copy of it was in existence, and Milton is known to have been interested in "Britannia's Pastorals." A copy of the folio edition of the latter poem in Mr. Huth's library is even thought to contain annotations by him.

It will be remembered that Milton did not give his masque the name it now bears; perhaps he was actuated both by modesty and by a desire to avoid the confusion of his poem with a Latin play entitled "Comus," written by a professor at Louvain, Hendrik van der Putten, or, as he was known to the scholarly world, Erycius Puteanus. This "extravaganza in prose and verse," as Masson calls it, had been printed in 1608, and an English edition had appeared at Oxford in 1634. I have not been able to see a copy of it, but I gather from the editors that it is not unlikely that Milton had seen the book and taken a few hints from it. Ben Jonson, too, in his masque, "Pleasure Reconciled to Virtue" (1619), had introduced Comus as a character, but only as "the god of cheer or the Belly." Milton could have got little inspiration from this "first father of sauce and deviser of jelly," whose personal appearance, though resembling that of our great Comus, was plainly derived from the "Imagines" of the elder Philostratus. The Comus of Puteanus is said to be "a much subtler embodiment of sensual hedonism"[1] than Jonson's belly-god, but all good critics are agreed that Milton's conception of the character is essentially his own, and that, in the words of his chief biographer, "he was bold enough to add a brand-new god, no less, to the classic Pantheon, and to import him into Britain." But it would seem that Puteanus ought at least to have the credit for having seen that the shadowy deity of the post-classical period could be developed into a figure of interest and importance.

We have now fairly described the extent of Milton's indebtedness to other writers, and it will be seen that he did no more than almost every other great poet has done—he appropriated and bettered. The plagiarist-hunter will therefore find little true profit in tracking him; but as this eccentric is usually harmless, it may be as well to amuse him by referring him not only to Spenser's description of "the Maske of Cupid" in the twelfth canto of the third book of "The Faërie Queene," but also to that stanza of the poem (II., xii., 56) in

[1] See Verity's introduction to his excellent edition of "Comus."

which a "comely dame" is represented as holding a cup of gold full of sappy liquor whereof

> "She used to give to drinke to each
> Whom passing by she happened to meet
> It was her guise all straungers goodly so to greet."

When these verses are compared with the passage in "Comus" containing the lines, —

> "Offering to every weary traveller
> His orient liquor in a crystal glass
> To quench the drouth of Phœbus," —

it ought to be as apparent that Spenser is the author of "Comus" as that Bacon is the author of the plays attributed to Shakspere.

But it is time to conclude, even though we must forego the pleasure of commenting upon particular passages of this exquisite poem. The reader who loves poetry will lose nothing through our silence, for such an one will need no critic to point out to him the abiding loveliness and beauty of the purest of English poems. "Comus" is great in the purity and beauty of its sentiments, in the depth and range of its underlying philosophy, in the nobility of its diction, and the fluidity of its rhythmical movement. It is not great structurally, and could not have maintained the grand style at its height; but this is only another way of saying that in 1634 Milton could not have written "Paradise Lost." The imperfect of a higher species may, however, be worth much more to us than the perfect of a lower species. Gray's "Elegy" is more perfect as a work of art than "Comus," and is beautiful in itself, but Milton's masque obviously represents a far higher poetical achievement.

CHAPTER V

THE ELEGIAC POEMS

WHILE Milton as the author of "Lycidas" and the "Epitaphium Damonis" is assuredly the greatest English elegist, it does not follow that he is the most typical. That honor is reserved for Gray. Milton seldom or never fails to lay the tender and melodious flute aside for a moment to give us more inspiring strains upon the trumpet or the lyre. This fact has given some purists occasion for inept criticism — especially with regard to "Lycidas." They seem to think that because the strictly elegiac note of lament (*querimonia*) is not kept throughout, the poem ceases to be harmonious, and hence to be a work of art. They forget that there is such a thing as fusion of diverse elements in art as well as in chemistry. A mechanical mixture of inharmonious elements will certainly not produce a work of art; a mechanical mixture of merely diverse but not necessarily inharmonious elements will certainly detract from, if not completely mar, a work of art. But a fusion of such diverse elements may, under favorable circumstances, produce a new form of artistic product, or modify an old and well-known form. The idyllists of Alexandria, while preserving the metre and some other features of the older and the newer epic, nevertheless, by the fusion of new elements, produced a separate and distinct form of poetry. The fusion of this form, the idyll, with the elegy, modified the older form, and produced what we know as the pastoral elegy. Whether now Milton was able to modify this last form and still preserve its artistic qualities and nature, is a question that must be discussed when we consider "Lycidas."

As we have seen, Milton's first elegiac was almost his first poetic effort. In the autumn of 1626, when he was not quite eighteen, his sister, Mrs. Anne Phillips, lost her first child, a daughter, and the young collegian lamented the event in the well-known poem, "On the Death of a Fair Infant, dying of a Cough." If it were not for the fact that such contentions are always unnecessary, because always incapable of settlement, one might well maintain that this is the most remarkable poem ever written by a boy of equal age. It seems to be even better than Lamb's famous and admirable lines "On an Infant dying as soon as born," and it is certainly better than Lovelace's "Elegy" on the Princess Katherine, "born, christened, buried in one day"—with both of which poems one naturally compares it. If it has not the subtle tenderness of Lamb's lines, it has a dignity and elevation worthy of the Milton of riper years. This elevation warrants certain writers in treating the poem as an ode. It is, indeed, an elegiac ode, complete in eleven of those modified rhyme-royal stanzas that have been already described, and it is one of the best English poems of its kind, although manifestly inferior to Dryden's masterpiece in the same class of composition, the splendid and imperishable "Ode to the Memory of Mrs. Anne Killigrew."

As has just been intimated, it is not difficult to trace in this youthful poem qualities that were never to be absent from Milton's work. There is the wonderful mastery of language and rhythm, the high seriousness, the free and unpedantic use of classical allusion, that have distinguished Milton as an artist from all other English poets. There is, it is true, as in most of the early poems, a marked leaning toward the Fantastic School, yet there is so much stateliness of manner that the extravagances are overlooked. But a quotation or two will obviate the necessity for further comment:—

"O fairest flower, no sooner blown but blasted,
Soft silken primrose fading timelessly"—

are verses that any poet, even the greatest, might be proud to call his own. The elevation proper to the ode form appears plainly in the following stanza, the fourth:—

"Yet art thou not inglorious in thy fate;
For so Apollo, with unweeting hand,
Whilom did slay his dearly-lovèd mate,
Young Hyacinth born on Eurotas' strand,
Young Hyacinth the pride of Spartan land;
But then transformed him to a purple flower;
Alack! that so to change thee Winter had no power."

Certainly there was no other poet living in Jacobean England save Ben Jonson who could have paralleled this stanza, nor in the quarter of a century to follow was there to be one capable of equalling it, although it was to be a period of considerable activity in the composition of elegiac verse. Perhaps, however, an exception to this statement must be made in favor of the eight immortal lines in which the great Marquis of Montrose poured forth the passion and the anguish of his soul at the execution of his royal master.

But Milton was soon to use his elegiac powers to better purpose than in this poem, or in the Latin elegies that will be discussed later. In 1630 he composed his splendid epitaph on Shakspere, thus fairly measuring his strength against Ben Jonson in the latter's strongest point. Although it hardly seems that the epitaph on "the admirable dramatic poet," which was published anonymously in the Second Folio of 1632, is equal in human appropriateness and in perfection of workmanship to the best of Jonson's epitaphs, such as that on Philip Gray, or that it is as important as a tribute to Shakspere's greatness as Jonson's famous memorial lines, still no one will deny that it is worthy to rank among the greatest of epitaphs and the greatest of tributes. It would be difficult to point out any verses of Dryden or Pope that excel in epigrammatic terseness and strength the closing couplet:—

"And so sepúlchered in such pomp dost lie,
That kings for such a tomb would wish to die."

About this time Milton wrote his humorous elegies on the death of Hobson, the Cambridge carrier, the well-known original of the expression "Hobson's choice." It is not easy to associate with Milton the idea of humor, at least of the fantastic sort displayed in these poems. But they do contain humor, although of a not very volatile kind. They are better than the somewhat similar verses written by Bishop Corbet on the manciple and butler of Christ Church, Oxford; but they are certainly not equal to Robert Fergusson's delightful elegy on John Hogg, porter to the University of St. Andrews.

In 1631 the young poet wrote an epitaph,

long enough to be an elegy, on the Marchioness of Winchester, who had been lamented by Jonson and others, and whose husband was to have the honor of an epitaph by Dryden. Singularly enough, as in the case of Chaucer and the Duchess of Lancaster, the poet was of exactly the same age as the subject of his verses — twenty-three. The epitaph, which is seventy-four verses long, is in that blending of seven- and eight-syllabled couplets which Milton borrowed from the Elizabethans like Barnfield, but of which he is so great a master. It is in many respects a true epitaph in spite of its length, and it has some of the characteristics of a requiem. As in the case of many other epitaphs of the period, the fact that the lady died in childbirth is given a prominence that seems unnecessary to our modern notions; but at least the poem is practically unmarred by conceits, although it is a typical product of the Cavalier muse of Milton's earlier years. The Puritan that was to be is foreshadowed, but only foreshadowed, in the exquisite comparison with Jacob's wife Rachel, and the classical touch is, of course, present also.

There is little in English poetry that marks a higher reach than the concluding verses; and the elegy as a whole, with all due regard to Mr. Swinburne's contrary opinion, is distinctly superior to Ben Jonson's lines upon the same lady.

Six years later, after the retirement at Horton had produced "Comus," Milton composed the crowning poem of his youth, the pastoral elegy "Lycidas."

The external facts relating to its evolution are ample on the whole, and easy to set forth. Among his friends at Christ's College had been two sons of Sir John King, long Secretary for Ireland. They were admitted during his third year, Roger, the elder, being sixteen, and his brother Edward two years younger. Nothing seems to be heard of them until four years later, when, to the surprise of every one, Edward King was chosen a Fellow of the College, in obedience to a royal mandate, which had doubtless been obtained through considerable political influence. Such royal interference was not usual or palatable, and it must have been especially galling to Milton, who, as a Bachelor of two years' standing and "an acknowledged ornament of his college," to quote Professor Masson, had good reason to expect that the honor would have fallen to him. He seems, however, to have taken his disappointment gracefully, and to have shared the general liking for his brilliant and amiable college-mate, who, thanks to the pen of his disappointed rival, now lives in our memories even more freshly than his two greater fellow-students, John Cleveland, the Royalist poet, and Henry More, the Platonist. After Milton left Cambridge, King continued his academic career in an orthodox and successful way, proceeding M.A. in 1633, and filling the offices of tutor and prælector while preparing himself for active work in the Church. During the vacation of 1637, however, he sailed from Chester for Ireland, where he had been born and where he had relations and friends of high social standing. On the 10th of August his ship struck on a rock off the Welsh coast, and went down. Accounts vary as to the cause of the accident, and it is not known how many, if any, were saved. The memorial volume shortly to be described states that he died in the act of prayer, which would imply that some of the passengers and crew escaped, but may be merely a touch of imagination.

When the news of King's death was received at Cambridge, it was at once felt that special steps should be taken to do honor to his memory, and at that time this laudable desire could be accomplished in no fitter way than by the publication of a volume of elegies inscribed with his name. The collection, when it finally appeared from the University Press, consisted of two parts, separately paged and titled, both bearing the date 1638. The first portion consisted of twenty-three poems in Greek and Latin, filling thirty-six pages. Both the learned languages figured in the title, which ran, *Justa Edovardo King naufrago ab amicis mœrentibus, amoris et μνείας χάριν*, or, as Masson once translated it, "Obsequies to Edward King, drowned by shipwreck, in token of love and remembrance, by his sorrowing friends"—which is only grammatically ambiguous. The second part consisted of thirteen English poems, filling twenty-five pages, and was entitled "Obsequies to the Memorie of Mr. Edward King, Anno Dom. 1638." Of the contributors we need note only Henry More, who naturally wrote in Greek; Henry King, Edward's brother; Joseph Beaumont, afterward author of a curious poem called "Psyche"; and John Cleveland, who subsequently showed his powers as an elegist when Charles I. was his subject, but here fell little short of the climax of absurdity.

"Lycidas" was, of course, included in Milton's 1645 edition of his poems, and the short prose argument which now precedes the verses was then inserted. No changes save orthographical were made in the edition of 1673; the version of 1645 is, therefore, the final form its author gave to his lyrical masterpiece. A comparison of the Cambridge Ms., the edition of 1638, and a copy of this edition, with corrections in Milton's handwriting, still preserved in the University Library at Cambridge, has enabled critics to trace the evolution of certain passages of the poem, and thrown much light upon Milton's habits of composition. Such investigation furnishes technical proof of what every capable critic would have surmised, that the poet was a meticulous artist, careful of word and phrase, and sure to better whatever he changed.

But it is time to consider "Lycidas" in its higher relations as a contribution to the world's small stock of supremely excellent poetry, and first of the artistic category to which it belongs. Milton himself termed it a "monody," which it is, save in the last eight lines; but we cannot read far in it without discovering that it is a pastoral poem as well. We are, therefore, induced to class it as a pastoral elegy, and to rank it with the famous elegiac idylls of Theocritus, Bion, Moschus, and Virgil, to say nothing of their modern imitators. Perhaps Milton was induced to give his elegy this form through the influence of Spenser, who had thus lamented the death of Sidney; but it is more likely that he was affected by the example of the great Alexandrian poets. As the pastoral is now an out-worn form of verse, it follows that "Lycidas" has been pronounced to be artificial and insincere, Dr. Johnson being the most stentorian exponent of this view; it will therefore be necessary for us to vindicate the fitness of the form Milton chose for his tribute, before we can proceed with our discussion of the poem itself.

That pastoral poetry is more or less artificial in character does not admit of doubt. The goatherds of Theocritus were, indeed, to some extent worthy of the exquisite poetry put in their mouths, and Theocritus himself may be regarded as naturalistic in comparison with his followers. But that the Roman and the modern European pastoral is to any appreciable extent naturalistic, is a position that only a very rash critic will assume. It does not follow, however, that pastoral poetry, because it is artificial and not naturalistic, is therefore to be tabooed as a form of art. All art has its conventions, and those of pastoral poetry are exceptional in degree rather than in kind. It is a convention when the dramatist makes his hero soliloquize in blank verse and in tragic vein — it is equally a convention when the pastoral elegist forgets his sheep and proceeds to bewail in tender elegiacs his mate who has passed to Proserpina's dark abode. But to preserve the well-recognized conventions of pastoral poetry, and at the same time refrain from stirring the reader's sense of the incongruous and the ridiculous, or from overtaxing his imagination and his sympathy by excessive artificiality, is an achievement that few poets have attained to. Yet that there have been successful pastoral poets and great pastoral poems is plain to any student of our literature who recalls the names of Spenser and Fletcher, and the titles "Lycidas" and "Thyrsis."

With regard now to the effect of the artificiality or conventionality of this class of poetry on the sincerity of the poet when he applies it to the expression of his personal sorrow, it is easy to see that a mediocre poet would either fail to write a true pastoral or else fail to show one spark of true feeling. A glance through the volumes of Chalmers will bring to light a number of frigid performances that will prove the truth of this assertion. But it often happens that a real poet succeeds best when the difficulties of his art-form are greatest. Hence it is that three of the finest of English elegies, "Lycidas," "Adonais," and "Thyrsis," are pastoral elegies. Nor will this seem curious when we remember that the restrained grief at the death of a dear relative or friend, which is due to the conventionalities of society, is often far more impressive than the wild and unrestrained grief indulged in on similar occasions by mourners in the lower ranks of life. If, however, any one is still in doubt on this point, let him compare with "Lycidas" two simple, *i.e.* non-pastoral, elegies written on friends drowned at sea — to wit, George Turberville's "Epitaph on Maister Arthur Brooke," and Propertius's elegy on Pætus. Making all allowances for Milton's greater genius, we can hardly fail to perceive the superiority of the more complex over the more simple form of lament.

But the critics frequently shift their point of attack from the capabilities of the pastoral form to express emotion to the sincerity of the grief felt by Milton himself. "Lycidas," they say, lacks sincerity, and hence fails to make a true appeal, because it has not and could not have had the note of personal sorrow that is found in such a poem as "In Memoriam." Arthur Hallam was Tennyson's bosom friend; Edward King had been promoted over Milton's head at college, and the latter did not even mention the sad drowning in the Irish Sea in two contemporary familiar letters to Diodati. But surely one does not need to be intimate with a man in order to be sincere in mourning his premature taking-off. Milton knew of King well enough, and he was aware that the latter was just the kind of man that was needed for the ministry of the Church. "Lycidas" itself is proof sufficient of the interest Milton took in that ministry, and of the scorn he had for its unworthy representatives; the poem is equal proof of the sincere grief its author felt for the loss of one whom he had known and admired, and whom he had believed destined to do a great work within the Christian fold. There was therefore in the relations of the two men scope for personal emotion of a high and pure kind, and this emotion was fused by Milton's artistic skill into a poem which, after a wide course of reading in the class of poetry to which it belongs, I have little hesitation in pronouncing to be the noblest elegy in any of the greater literatures. If it is not sincere, then I am at a complete loss to account for the true ring of such supremely flawless verses as—

> "For Lycidas is dead, dead ere his prime,
> Young Lycidas, and hath not left his peer,"

or

> "But, oh! the heavy change now thou art gone,
> Now thou art gone and never must return,"

or

> "Ay me! I fondly dream
> 'Had ye been there,' . . . for what could that have done?"

or

> "It was that fatal and perfidious bark,
> Built in the eclipse, and rigged with curses dark,
> That sunk so low that sacred head of thine,"

or, finally, the whole passage beginning

> "Ay me! whilst thee the shores and sounding seas
> Wash far away"

and ending

> "And, O ye dolphins, waft the hapless youth."

It may be, indeed, merely my own imagination that discovers in these verses a note of personal sorrow. Read casually they perhaps strike one as being beautiful only, but read and re-read, and studied word by word, they reveal that deep, underlying sincerity that must be the basis of all perfect art. Grief worked up for the occasion, or the general concern one feels at hearing of the death of a brilliant college-mate, never inspired such verses or such a poem. I could as soon be persuaded that Shakspere did not, partially at least, "unlock his heart" in his divine sonnets as that Milton did not unlock his heart in the equally flawless and divine verses I have just quoted. Flawless art, I repeat, presupposes the deepest sincerity, and I am bold enough or eccentric enough to maintain that there are verses in "Lycidas" in which Milton has, consciously or unconsciously, struck as deep a note of personal sorrow as has ever been struck by an English poet. One can naturally no more prove such an assertion than one can prove that the late Professor Minto was mistaken in his theory that the second series of Shakspere's "Sonnets" represents a sort of satiric fancy rather than a genuine passion for a fascinating woman. All one can say is, that if flawless art "plays such fantastic tricks before high heaven," it is indeed enough to make the angels weep.

Turning now to the question of the particular poems that may have influenced Milton in writing "Lycidas," we must give the first place to the three great pastoral elegies of the Alexandrians — to the "Song of Daphnis" in the First Idyll of Theocritus, to the "Song of Adonis" of Bion, and the "Lament for Bion" by Moschus. To these should be added the Fifth and Tenth Eclogues of Virgil.

I cannot see that Propertius's beautiful elegy on Pætus or Ovid's on Tibullus was at all in Milton's mind. Critics have cited such modern pastorals as the "Alcon" of the Italian poet Castiglione as having been drawn on for imagery, but I can discover nothing that both poets could not easily have derived from their common sources of inspiration. This seems to be true of Marot's pastoral on the death of Louise of Savoy, and of the eclogue that Spenser modelled on it. The latter poet's "Astrophel" may have had a slight stylistic influence; but even this much can hardly be said of Ludovick Bryskett's poor pastoral on

Sidney, in spite, as we shall see presently, of the claims put forward for it by Dr. Guest. Nor can I think that the pretty elegies and dirges of William Browne of Tavistock were specially in Milton's mind when he wrote, although more than one critic has traced the influence of Browne. It is true that Milton was a reader of Browne, and it is also true that Browne lamented in a touching way the death of a drowned friend; but these facts do not prove conscious imitation. Turberville's epitaph on Arthur Brooke, the translator of "Romeo and Juliet," who perished by shipwreck in a way that reminds one strikingly of the death of King, has, in spite of a certain crudity, more in common with "Lycidas" than Browne's laments have. The stanza with the pathetic invocation to Arion's dolphin brings up immediately one of the finest lines in "Lycidas," but it would be rash to affirm that the stanza gave birth to the line. In short, it is easy to conclude that "Lycidas" is unique among modern elegies, whether preceding or following; for it would be hard to trace any marked influence exerted by it on "Adonais" or "Thyrsis."

But while we can easily dismiss Milton's relations to modern pastoral poets, we should say a word here about the way he treated his Alexandrian masters. In the first place, he followed Virgil in dropping the refrain. Secondly, he made little or no attempt in "Lycidas" to paint any of those pretty but elaborate little pictures that gave idyllic poetry its name. For the beautiful invocation to the nymphs (ll. 50–62) he was indebted to Theocritus rather than to Virgil's Tenth Eclogue; but his substitution of British for classical names was a proof at once of his patriotism and of his invariable habit and power of bettering what he condescended to borrow. Unlike Moschus, he saw no reason to reserve to the last the expression of his personal sorrow, and it is needless to say that the hopelessness of the Greek in the presence of death found no place in his verses.

The influence of his classical models on particular lines and phrases of "Lycidas" is too apparent to require much notice. The name "Lycidas" itself and those of Damœtas, Amaryllis, and Neæra are, of course, borrowed from these sources. The references to the hyacinth "inscribed with woe," to the grief of the flowers for Lycidas's death, to the mournful echoes of the caves, all suggest the Alexandrian idylls; and Milton himself confesses the source of much of his inspiration by his invocation to "fountain Arethuse" and "smooth-sliding Mincius," and by his expression "Doric lay." Minute commentators have even shown that he has been misled into making the Hebrus a swift river through his reliance upon a phrase in Virgil which is supposed to be a misreading. But "Lycidas" has a beauty and passion unknown to its Alexandrian predecessors, and it has not a touch of their oriental effeminacy and licentiousness.

Something must now be said about the marvellous rhythm of the poem. The iambic pentameter is the prevailing line, but trimeters and tetrameters are irregularly introduced throughout with exquisite effect. The rhythm is varied, and flows now in leaping waves, now in long rolling billows that carry all before them, like the surging periods of "Paradise Lost." There is probably no short poem in the language the rhythm of which has been more deservedly praised and studied, or more despaired of by other poets. Milton's mastery of rhythm, remarkable from the first, almost culminated in "Lycidas," in spite of the fact that he was there subjected (practically for the last time) to what he afterward called "the troublesome and modern bondage of riming." There is nothing in the unrhymed (or rhymed) portions of "Comus" that, to my ear, at all equals in majesty and splendor of rhythmical movement the passage in "Lycidas" that begins

"Ay me! whilst thee the shores and sounding seas"—

and perhaps there is nothing in "Paradise Lost" that excels it. But it is the rhymed structure of "Lycidas" that has attracted most attention, because it is almost unique. Three of its notable peculiarities may be pointed out. In the 193 verses there are 10 that have no rhyming relations with others in their vicinity. There is no fixed order of rhyme, and where, as often happens, two adjacent verses rhyme, they sometimes fail to form a couplet in the strict sense of the word. There is a paucity of rhymed endings (only about 60 in the poem) which shows that one sound and its related rhymes do duty for several verses; *e.g.* ll. 2, 5, 6, 9, 12, 14, end respectively with "sere," "year," "dear," "peer," "bier," and "tear." Other peculiarities, such as the use of assonance, might be dwelt upon, but the reader may observe these for himself, for the main question that concerns us here is, How did these peculiarities originate? This question was long ago indirectly answered by Dr. Johnson, when, in the course of his famous "Life," he casually remarked on the fact that Milton's "mixture of longer and shorter verses, according to the rules of Tuscan poetry," proved his "acquaintance with the Italian writers." Later Dr. Guest tried to show that an irregularly rhymed pastoral by Ludovick Bryskett on the death of Sidney (which made no use of verses without rhyme or of varying length) had been in Milton's mind when he wrote "Lycidas"; but that our great poet was influenced by the Italian masters, both in his arrangement of rhymes and in his alternation of shorter and longer verses, will be apparent to any one who will take the trouble to analyze the choruses of the "Aminta" or "Il Pastor Fido," or to examine a treatise on Italian metres.[1]

The reader will already have gathered that there has been much difference of opinion with regard to the merits of "Lycidas." Dr. Johnson wound up his curiously inept criticism by remarking: "Surely no man could have fancied that he read 'Lycidas' with pleasure had he not known the author." The cold and judicious Hallam wrote on the other hand: "It has been said, I think very fairly, that 'Lycidas' is a good test of real feeling for what is peculiarly called poetry."[2] Mark Pattison practically regarded "Lycidas" as the greatest poem in the language. Dr. Garnett dissents from this view, holding that the

[1] Mr. Verity notes that Landor also saw Milton's metrical obligations to Tasso and Guarini, and refers to the English critic's collected works (1876), iv., 499.

[2] "I have been reading 'Comus' and 'Lycidas' with wonder, and a sort of awe. Tennyson once said that 'Lycidas' was a touchstone of poetic taste." — EDWARD FITZGERALD to Fanny Kemble, March 26, 1880.

beauties of the poem are exquisite rather than magnificent, and that as an elegy it has been surpassed by "Adonais." It seems hard to justify this criticism. Both poems contain exquisite passages, and both contain magnificent passages, but I know of nothing in "Adonais" that is so exquisite as the flower passage in "Lycidas," or so magnificent as the speech of St. Peter, or the picture of the corpse of Lycidas washed by "the shores and sounding seas." Then, again, it seems plain that Milton understood better than Shelley the nature of the art form in which they purposed to cast their thoughts. Shelley's mind was too hazy to enable him to reproduce the pellucid beauty of his Greek originals, and his personifications, though not wanting in power, were far from clear-cut. This is not saying, of course, that the "Adonais" is not a great poem, or that it has not a greater historical interest than "Lycidas," and after all any literature may well be proud of possessing two such elegies.

The mention of the speech of St. Peter reminds us, however, that it and the other "higher mood" concerned with Apollo and true fame have given the critics much trouble because they do not seem to be in keeping with the plaintive tone of the normal elegy.

The question therefore arises — "Was Milton necessarily committing an artistic blunder when he introduced into his pastoral elegy elements that at first sight seem foreign to it?" This question had practically been answered long before by Virgil and those of his successors who had used the pastoral for political and other similar purposes, but we may answer it for ourselves after a brief discussion of the two passages in "Lycidas" that have excited so much animadversion.

With the first, beginning

"Alas! what boots it with uncessant care,"

less fault has been found. The transition is not too abrupt, and the nobility and beauty of the verses would almost justify their insertion, even if they did not follow naturally on the mention of Orpheus — the son of the muse — who perished at the hands of the ignoble throng. They are not, it is true, the soft complaints of a courtly lover masquerading as a shepherd, nor are they the exquisite wail of a jaded, *fin-de-siècle* balladist who has retired from the world to lament in disgust the interest men take in everything except his fragile poetry. They are rather the last deep sigh that Milton's noble bosom will permit itself before, in the consciousness of a high and pure purpose, it is bared to the assaults of an alien and pitiless world. But to ask that an elegist shall not sigh so deeply is like insisting that no greater poet than a Tibullus shall ever touch the elegiac flute, and proclaiming that there is no room in our poetic hierarchy for a Propertius.

It is the second exalted passage introducing St. Peter mourning over the degeneracy of the English Church that has caused our solicitous critics most pain. The introduction of Triton, the message of Æolus, even the episode of the river Cam were allowable enough in such a pastoral; but why, ask the critics, should the bucolic poet turn preacher? Why should he blend with his shepherd's pipe the trumpet of the prophet, even though he blow it with the might of an archangel? Perhaps the fact that

Milton himself saw no incongruity in his procedure will seem a sufficient answer to those of us who believe that what Shakspere or Milton have joined together no man should lightly put asunder. But objectors will not be satisfied with this; so we may tell them that by his infusion of passion and scorn Milton, like Shelley in "Adonais," has given an intensity of tone to his elegy which even Moschus failed to give to his heartfelt lament for Bion. He has given it a higher spiritual significance than Propertius, with all his sincerity and power, could give to his lines on Pætus. He has broken loose from the restraints of the pastoral form just where one direct passionate outburst was needed to give the proper contrast, and so to heighten the effect, just as the single sigh or groan that escapes from a strong, self-contained mourner is supreme in its effect, and appears to emphasize, not only the grief he is enduring, but also the strength with which, except for one bare instant, he has controlled that grief. The passage is another crowning proof of Milton's power of blending the characteristics of Greek and Hebrew, and it is natural enough when the conditions of the time are taken into account. If Cambridge could be represented as mourning in person the death of King as a scholar, surely St. Peter could mourn with equal propriety the death of King as an intended priest. With regard to the details of the speech put into St. Peter's mouth, there cannot be two opinions. For concentrated scorn, and awful, mysterious power and import, the speech has no equal. It is to be noted further that Milton successfully adapts pastoral language to his high purposes, and that he manages the transition from the higher to the lower "moods" with consummate felicity. If these claims are justified, we are in a position to assert that Milton, by his fusion of the intensity of the true ode with the idyllic beauty and tender pathos of the pastoral elegy proper, has modified and improved an old and established form of art. But one could write about "Lycidas" forever and not exhaust the subject, so it will be as well to cry a halt and to pass to a brief consideration of the Latin elegies that culminate in the "Epitaphium Damonis," leaving to one side the two sonnets of an elegiac cast, which cannot well be considered apart from their companion poems in this specially elaborate verse-form.

The Latin elegies will not demand much attention because, with the exception of the "Epitaphium Damonis," they do not differ in quality from the youthful exercises already examined. Two poems in the "Elegiarum Liber" are true elegies — viz. the second written at the age of seventeen on the death of the Cambridge beadle, and the third written about the same time on the death of the Bishop of Winchester. Even if they had been done in English, they would have been remarkable as the work of a schoolboy; in their flowing Latin they are even more remarkable, although obviously academical in tone and matter. It is not a little curious that the future Puritan should in his youth have celebrated the deaths of two prelates in apparently sincere effusions. The tribute to the Bishop of Winchester contains a short description of the flight of the angels bearing the soul of the bishop to heaven which suggests comparison with Cowley's similar verses with regard to Crashaw. The advantage lies with Cowley, but the boyish dream of St. Cuthbert touches us more than the vision of either poet.

The first poem of the collection entitled "Sylvarum Liber" is an ode in alcaics lamenting the death of the Vice-Chancellor, a physician. It too was written in Milton's seventeenth year, and is creditable to his genius in spite of its classical commonplaces. The next poem but one of the same collection is the second of the prelatical elegies, being an ode in iambic trimeters on the death of the Bishop of Ely. This tribute was written shortly after that to the Bishop of Winchester, and in it the Prelate himself makes a long speech which contains a good description of the passage of his soul through the stars.

But it is the last of Milton's Latin elegies, the famous "Epitaphium Damonis," that alone demands serious consideration.

This is a pastoral following the Alexandrian pattern more closely than does "Lycidas," and, as was natural, it is a tenderer poem than the latter. In poetic beauty it ranks above all Milton's elegiac verse except "Lycidas"; and, indeed, above most of the elegies ever written by Englishmen. It has been frequently pointed out that the great merit of Milton's Latin verse, when at its best, lies not in its technical skill, although that is great, but in the fact that the foreign medium cannot obscure the intense feeling of the poet. This is abundantly shown in the "Epitaphium Damonis," which is so great a poem that one can but regret, with Mr. Pattison, that being in Latin it is unfortunately "inaccessible to uneducated readers."

Like its Alexandrian and Roman models it is written in hexameters, and not in the elegiac couplet. It has the refrain

> "Ite domum impasti, domino iam non vacat, agni."[1]

It begins by invoking the Sicilian nymphs, and by recalling the elegies on Daphnis and Bion. It abounds in classical names and allusions, and is minutely pastoral in its language and incidents — much more so than "Lycidas." Lastly, and especially, it follows its models by showing the proper idyllic touch

[1] Thus rendered by Cowper: —

> "Go, seek your home, my lambs; my thoughts are due
> To other cares than those of feeding you."

—the imitation of the Alexandrian pictorial masters in the exquisite description of the goblets ("pocula") given to the poet by his Neapolitan friend Manso. The strain of personal loss is present throughout, especially in the pathetic lines in which Milton's visit to Rome is deplored because it kept him from the bedside of his friend; and although there are no such rises to "higher moods" as in "Lycidas," we are gratified by such autobiographical touches as the lines that tell us of the contemplated abandonment of Latin verse as a vehicle of expression, and of the proposed Arthurian epic mentioned also in "Mansus," which, alas! was never written. In fine, the "Epitaphium Damonis" is a great pastoral elegy, in which Milton fused his love and knowledge of the classics with his love for Diodati and England, and with his noble sense of his own high mission, into a poem which ought to be studied even if one has to learn Latin in order to read it. "Fictitious bucolicism" the poem may exhibit, but, in the words of Mr. Pattison, this "is pervaded by a pathos which, like volcanic heat, has fused into a new compound the dilapidated débris of the Theocritean world."

Particular criticism is probably unnecessary, but I may suggest a comparison of the closing lines descriptive of Diodati's reception in Paradise with the similar close of "Lycidas," and I cannot forbear pointing out the pathos and felicity of these verses:—

"Vix sibi quisque parem de millibus invenit unum,
Aut si sors dederit tandem non aspera votis,
Illum inopina dies, qua non speraveris hora,
Surripit, æternum linquens in sæcula damnum."

These have been Englished by Cowper as follows:—

"We scarce in thousands meet one kindred mind,
And if the long-sought good at last we find,
When least we fear it, Death our treasure steals,
And gives our heart a wound that nothing heals."

But the only man to translate these lines properly was Milton himself.

The "Epitaphium Damonis" was not only Milton's last important Latin poem; it was also, as we have seen, his last real elegy. In the turmoil of public and the sorrows of private life, his mighty spirit was to find other and higher work to perform for "the great Task-master's eye." That work will be spoken of in the chapters that follow; here the hope may be expressed that no reader will suffer himself to be so dazzled by the splendor of the poetical achievements of Milton's old age (and dazzled he will be if he approach it with a mind trained in the principles of sound criticism and unaffected by the shallow and uncultured revolt against classical standards of excellence that is so rife at present) as to be blind to the charm, the blended grace and power that mark the noble poems of his youth. Great even to sublimity is the Milton of "Paradise Lost,"

> "from the cheerful ways of men,
> Cut off."

Great, too, and matchless in charm is the Milton of "Lycidas,"

> "With eager thought warbling his Doric lay."

CHAPTER VI

THE PROSE WORKS

Quite recently Mr. Gosse, in his admirable short history of English literature, has expressed a doubt whether people really can admire Milton's prose. Some years ago Mr. Lowell declared that his prose had "no style, in the higher sense"; that his sentences were often "loutish and difficult"; that he was careless of euphony; that he too often blustered, *et cetera.* Nearly all critics have admitted the splendor of his best passages, but have hastened immediately to qualify their praises by animadverting upon his clumsy syntax, his lack of coherence, his coarseness, his malignity, his want of humor, and the like. Most of these charges have, indeed, a basis of truth, which makes them difficult to refute; but like much other current criticism they do their object gross injustice. In reality Milton is a great prose writer, perhaps the greatest in our literature; but his greatness will never emerge from criticism that is chiefly negative. It may be a rash claim to make, yet I will be bold enough to maintain that, when all allowances are made, the prose works of Milton contain the noblest and most virile English that can be found in our literature, and that this is true, not merely of detached passages of the "Areopagitica" alone, but of the mass of his writings. Such a claim cannot, of course, be made good here or elsewhere; but it will be disputed with a positiveness inversely proportional to the disputants' study of Milton's controversial tracts.[1]

The phrase just used contains in itself many of the reasons for Milton's failure to take his proper rank as a prose writer. As a rule Milton wrote as a prose pamphleteer and advocate, and neither his matter nor his manner is calculated to please readers whose minds, indurated by preconception and prejudice, cannot play about the subjects he discusses. A partisan of

[1] Unless, of course, the critic has a theory to prove, as was Mr. Pattison's case, who, in his treatment of the prose works, is distinctly biassed.

the Stuarts, a devotee of liturgies, a reader of over-delicate sensibilities, will be almost certainly unable to judge Milton fairly. Even those who agree with him in religious and political matters will be generally incapable of getting rid of the effects of their present environment and dealing with him with that sympathy which is absolutely indispensable to all true criticism. As manners have improved, controversy has ceased to please; therefore it requires considerable effort to shake off our prepossessions sufficiently to get the proper æsthetic effect of Milton's writings. If, however, we can imagine ourselves fighting for an ideal state and an ideal religion, rejoicing in overcoming a doughty adversary, advocating liberty of thought and expression, promulgating a new system of education, — in short, if we can make ourselves ideal partisans of some great cause, we shall then be able to delight, not merely in Milton's exalted passages, but in the general vigor of his style, in the weight and dignity of his learning, in his thunderous wrath, in the sharpness of his satire, in the marvellous variety and abundance of his vocabulary, and in the thoroughly direct and masculine tone of his thought. In other words, we must steep ourselves in the Miltonic spirit before we can begin to realize how far Milton surpasses all competitors in strength and nobility as well as how far he possesses other qualities of style, such as charm and lucidity, usually denied him. We shall surely not comprehend him if we attempt to judge him from the "Areopagitica" or from a volume of specimens; yet it is to be feared that this is what many critics have unhesitatingly done.

The prose writings divide themselves naturally and easily into four groups. First, the five anti-prelatical tracts of 1641–1642; secondly, the four divorce tracts of 1643–1645; thirdly, the political pamphlets from 1649–1660, eleven in number unless the "Areopagitica" be added to make the full dozen; fourthly, the miscellanies, including the letters, state and private, the Grammar and the Logic, the histories of Britain and Muscovy, the "De Doctrina Christiana," and another ecclesiastical pamphlet, the letter to Hartlib on Education, and one or two short and unimportant publications.

These four groups we may now characterize briefly.

The titles of the ecclesiastical tracts are not alluring, running as they do: "Of Reformation touching Church Discipline in England," "Of Prelatical Episcopacy," "Animadversions upon the Remonstrant's Defence against Smectymnuus," "The Reason of Church Government urg'd against Prelaty," "Apology against a Pamphlet called A Modest Confutation of the Animadversions, etc." The form in which their author gave them to the world is no more alluring. They will always be heavy pamphlets, for even the resources of the modern printer cannot prevail against long paragraphs and defective chapter divisions. Yet it may be doubted whether seven more glorious paragraphs can be found in literature than those that close the first tract, or whether there is extant a more superb autobiographical passage than that contained in the preface to the second book of the "Reason of Church Government urg'd against Prelaty."

It is obviously impossible to analyze these pamphlets here, but it may be remarked that a careful study of them reveals the fact that Milton is more at home in historical and scholarly disquisitions than in the practical application of his principles, which are always of a root and branch order. Being an idealist, he cannot compromise; being Milton, he is absolutely regardless of consequences. But he is none the less a weighty and well-girt reasoner. Even when he is dealing with such a scholar as Archbishop Usher, he proves himself no mean antagonist in his use of patristic learning, and against Bishop Hall he is actually nimble to the point of indecorousness in his movements. He ascends and descends all the grades of partisanship from that of the prophet to that of the scolding fishwife; but perhaps only in one instance, that unfortunate one of the episcopal hose, does he cease entirely to be the powerful advocate of a dignified cause.

That cause — the cutting off of episcopacy and the approximation of the English Church to that of Geneva — may not appeal to many of us now, but has little to do with the power of Milton's style. The subject is at least as interesting as that of Bossuet's most famous funeral oration, and if the style is great and we are lovers of style, we should surely take the time to read the tracts. But what of the style?— for we may discuss it as fittingly in connection with these pamphlets, which exhibit it fully, as we should be able to do on completing the total body of the prose writings.

As we have seen, many of the charges brought against Milton's prose style must be partly admitted. He is turgid, but he is also past master of the potent phrase. Not only his sentences, but often his paragraphs, are loose because he does not pay sufficient attention to such an elementary matter as the unity of subject. But this general looseness of structure corresponds, of course, with Milton's looseness of thought, which in turn is due not to his lack of logic or power of cogent reasoning — he can be as logical and cogent as he pleases — but to the fulness of his erudition and to the main purpose of his controversial writings, *i.e.* to his design to overwhelm his adversaries and sweep away his readers by the mass and volume of his utterance. It is a great mistake to suppose that Milton did not know how to use the short sentence, or that he was unacquainted with the advantage of the English over the Latin idiom for the purposes of the writer who aims at a swift and strong expression of his ideas. Much of his prose is anything but the stiff, splendidly brocaded texture that many of the critics lay stress on; much of it is anything but the loose, interminably flowing robe with which many of us imagine that he continually enfolded himself. The fact is that Milton's prose structure, like his poetic, constantly impresses the student with its variety and mobility. His diction, too, is at times far from stiff, pedantic, and Latinistic, although his profound Latin studies plainly influenced it. I know of no English writer, unless it be Shakspere, who gives one such a sense of a copious, nay, inexhaustible, vocabulary. Perhaps this is due, as critics have remarked, to rapidity of circulation rather than to the actual quantity of different words employed; but it is the effect, not the cause, that concerns us, and the effect is that of an almost unbounded affluence of words. From the lowest grade of the scurrilous and vulgar, up to the most technically erudite and poetically sonorous of terms, his range is free and sovereign. He can scold like a shrew, he can discourse like an archangel; and if he indulges too much in the first rôle, owing to the temper of his times, and often to the nature of his task and the character of his adversary, we should never forget that he is the only mortal man who has ever been able to bear the weight of the second. This, I think, is his chief distinction — whether in his prose or in his poetry he is the noblest of writers. I will go farther and say that in his prose he is the most overwhelmingly strong of writers, and that I am bound to prefer superlative nobility and strength to all other qualities of style, or the sum of them. Critics like Mark Pattison may set Hooker above him for one reason and Bacon for another; but neither Hooker, nor Bacon, nor Jeremy Taylor, nor Sir Thomas Browne (whom Lowell avouches in this connection), nor any subsequent writer of English, gives me the sense of sublime power and variety and nobility — of eloquence in its highest meaning, that possesses me when I read the prose of Milton. Regular it is not, in the way that we properly demand of modern prose with its multiplicity of duties; it has not the clarity, the neatness, the precision of the French; it does not combine subtle charm and picturesqueness and brilliancy as does the prose of a writer like Châteaubriand; but it is better than all this, better than the stately periods of De Quincey or the regal march of Gibbon, better than the vigor of Macaulay or the beauty of Ruskin or the quiet force of Newman — it is either the utterance of a demigod or the speech of an angel.[1]

[1] It is not to be expected that the above praise will be deemed less than dithyrambic by any reader who has not fairly soaked himself in Milton's prose; neither is it to be expected that I should analyze the prose writings here in order to try to prove my point, or that readers who desire to investigate for themselves will be easily induced to study them in their present unattractive and almost inaccessible or rather *inabordable* form. Under these circumstances I shall resort to the expedient of referring in this lengthy note to certain passages of the tractate "Of Reformation," which more or less bear out some of the contentions made above.

The twentieth paragraph of Book I. contains six short sentences with the cumulative effect Macaulay used to aim at. It should be noticed in this connection that Milton's wide use of the relative is one of the chief syntactical reasons for his obscurity, and that frequently his sentences are long only because of faulty punctuation. A little familiarity with his style will, however, speedily minimize the effects of these hindrances.

The matter of Milton's second group of tracts is probably as little attractive to most people as that of his first, nor is his manner

That Milton could use vigorous, unpoetic, nay, unacademic English when he chose, is plain from such sentences or portions of sentences as these: —

The bishops "suffered themselves to be the common stales, to countenance with their prostituted gravities every politic fetch that was then on foot."

"It was not of old that a conspiracy of bishops could frustrate and fob off the right of the people."

"So have they hamstrung the valor of the subject by seeking to effeminate us all at home."

Such sentences could be multiplied indefinitely, but not more so than noble passages. The close of the whole tract has been referred to in the text, but one never knows when Milton is going to break out into a sublime strain, or indeed into some exquisite collocation of sounds like the following, which makes one smile at Mr. Lowell's remark about the lack of euphony: "But he [God], when we least deserved, sent out a gentle gale and message of peace from the wings of those his cherubims that fan his mercy-seat." The New England critic might, one would think, have hesitated to set up his ear against Milton's, if only in gratitude for the following sentences about his ancestors: —

"Next what numbers of faithful and free-born Englishmen, and good Christians, have been constrained to forsake their dearest home, their friends and kindred, whom nothing but the wide ocean, and the savage deserts of America, could hide and shelter from the fury of the bishops. O sir, if we could but see the shape of our dear mother England, as poets are of reasoning much more convincing. In his "Of Reformation" he had been guilty of arguing that because St. Martin had, after his elevation to the episcopate, complained of a loss of spiritual power, therefore God plainly had taken a "displeasure" at "an universal rottenness and gangrene in the whole [episcopal] function." In his divorce tracts he was capable of arguing for almost unlimited freedom of divorce, with scarcely a mention of the evils that would ensue to the family thus broken up. Yet neither in his precipitant inference from one particular to the general, nor in his selfish presentation of the divorce question from the man's point of view alone, was Milton other than his impetuous, whole-souled

wont to give a personal form to what they please, how would she appear, think ye, but in a mourning weed, with ashes upon her head and tears abundantly flowing from her eyes to behold so many of her children exposed at once, and thrust from things of dearest necessity, because their conscience could not assent to things which the bishops thought indifferent."

Do we not here, and in countless other passages, find Milton standing, to make use of his own noble words, on "one of the highest arcs, that human contemplation circling upwards can make from the globy sea whereon she stands"?

self. He was incapable of intellectual dishonesty of any conscious kind. He merely saw certain phases of his subject and pressed them home. He believed thoroughly in the depravity of bishops, and he felt deeply the need of some greater freedom in marriage, hence it never occurred to him that his methods of arguing could be pronounced disingenuous or misleading. He was a zealous Protestant, and therefore an individualist, that is, a more or less strenuous but not very cautious reasoner. Yet it is idle to maintain the attitude of those critics who seem to think that Milton's reasoning in ecclesiastical, social, and political matters was chiefly "sound and fury," or that it is impossible for latter-day readers to comprehend and sympathize with the positions taken by him. It would be truer to say that his positions are always intelligible, if not always sound, that his power as a writer is almost beyond praise, and his character one that none can comprehend without respect and admiration.

The best of the divorce tracts is the first, "The Doctrine and Discipline of Divorce."

The second, "The Judgment of Martin Bucer concerning Divorce," consists mainly of translations from the Latin of this eminent Protestant divine of the age of Edward VI., and of Milton's comments thereupon. "Tetrachordon," as its name imports, is a commentary on the four chief passages in Scripture treating of marriage and its annulment, while "Colasterion" is likewise self-explanatory in its title, as it is devoted to excoriating certain persons who had been rash enough to censure Milton for his "licentious" opinions. The two last-named pamphlets may be safely passed over by the general reader, for the first, although calm and dignified, is dry through the nature of the subject and the method of its treatment; and the second does not afford a fair measure of the vigor with which Milton could expound his principles, although it does give a fair idea of his ability to hector an adversary. But the reader who fails to read the first tract will fail to understand Milton in his capacity as an ideal reformer regardless of consequences. His motives were much less likely to be misunderstood in the episcopal controversy and in the Royalist muddle than in his attack upon indissoluble marriages; but Milton was of all men who ever lived the most resolute to follow his mind whithersoever it might carry him. He never went so far as to doubt the prime necessity of Scriptural warrant, or to cease to rely upon ancient, especially classical, precedents; but this fact, while it necessarily militates against the present currency of his ecclesiastical and political writings, should not blind us to the further facts, that for his time he was a most liberal thinker, and that no age has ever produced a more ideal one. It is this bold ideality that forms a basis, as it were, to his eloquence, which from now on prompts him to appeal in clarion tones either to the Parliament or the English people or the world at large. These appeals, whether in prefaces, as is the case with the first two divorce tracts, or in a special plea like the "Areopagitica," or in scattered passages, as frequently in the political works, furnish in the main the noble prose on which we have laid such stress; the strong prose is furnished by the body of nearly every book or pamphlet that proceeded from his pen.[1]

The ideality of the divorce tracts, which is seen not merely in Milton's fearless plea for individual liberty, but in his constant assertion that in marriage the mind counts for more than the body, is manifested just as strikingly in the nobly suggestive if impracticable "Of Education," and in the far more effective "Areopagitica," which through the irony of fate is almost the only thing that keeps him alive as a prose writer. The latter tract, superb as it is, does not contain his noblest work; nor perhaps does it represent his hammering vigor, his impetuous flow, as well as "The Tenure of Kings and Magistrates" and the "First Defence" do, or his compact strength as well as "Eikonoklastes" does. Still, it is so splendid that one is almost content, as is the case with Gray's "Elegy," not to attempt to disturb the public in a prepossession so creditable to it.

[1] In addition to the prefaces the reader should study also Chapters III. and VI. of the "Doctrine and Discipline." Chapters VIII. and XVII. show how subtle Milton's reasoning could be at times.

Passing now to the more specifically political tracts, it must suffice to say of the "Tenure" that it is admirably sincere and straightforward, — that it fairly throbs with the heart-beats of an ideal son of liberty, — but that it might well be more succinct in its logic and more true to the promise of its title. Milton does not show that it is lawful "for *any* who have the power" to put a tyrant to death, but he thunders splendidly against tyrants and turncoat Presbyterians, though not personally abusing Charles I., and gives ample proof of his own sincerity and courage. In "Eikonoklastes" he undertakes a harder piece of work, but one in which he is far more successful, in my judgment, than most critics have allowed. He had to answer, chapter by chapter, a book believed by thousands to have been written by a martyred king — a book which was practically a last will and testament. He is usually represented as having done it in a "savage" manner, — even Professor Masson allows himself to use the term, — but this is quite questionable. It would be idle to argue that Milton treated Charles gently, but I am inclined to think that he held himself in — a hard task — and that his general treatment of the king and his book was little more than warrantably sarcastic and severe, it being of course impossible for him then, or for some of us now, to look upon Charles as other than an evasive and dangerous foe. Milton was practically a republican, and most of his subsequent critics have been tinctured with monarchical prepossessions, hence his attitude toward Charles has seldom been fairly presented. Probably Richard Baron, who reissued "Eikonoklastes" in 1756, went too far in his praises of it, but it is certainly a performance of remarkable vigor and level strength — perhaps on the whole the most uniformly powerful of Milton's prose works. The arrangement as a commentary mars the modern reader's pleasure, and some of the arguments are both tedious and weak, but it was no credit to Milton's contemporaries that the book had so little temporary or permanent effect.[1]

[1] The general vigor of style and matter is seen clearly in Section VIII. Section X. contains some excellent sarcasm. Milton, it may be remarked, may not have lambent humor, but

The pamphlet devoted to the treaty made by the Earl of Ormond with the Irish rebels hardly deserves our notice, although the Presbytery of Belfast must have wished in their secret hearts that Milton had been otherwise employed than in writing it; but we cannot afford to be so summary in our treatment of the Reply to Salmasius and the two treatises that grew out of it. The moral grandeur displayed by Milton in preferring to lose his sight rather than that his beloved and then to him glorious England should go undefended, has been sufficiently praised elsewhere. It may be as well, however, to remark that this sacrifice of Milton's is not a figment of the imagination of his worshippers, but is attested to

he possesses an abundance of the thunder-bolt order. For grim, strong, hitting-the-mark shafts of scorn he has few or no rivals. Section XXIV. is an example of the effects of that weakness which almost invariably attends strong prejudices. Section XXV. toward the close shows a lack of charity distressing to modern notions; but Sections XXVII. and XXVIII., which conclude the book, are strong and dignified. It is worth while to notice that the so-called attack on Shakspere in Section I. has been entirely misread, and that, except when he engages in virulent personal controversy, there is little occasion for Milton's readers to fault the taste displayed in the prose works.

by himself in that splendid autobiographical passage which gives "The Second Defence of the People of England" its chief value. As for the general qualities of style and matter to be discovered in the "First Defence" or Reply to Salmasius, in the "Second Defence," and in the more specific attack on Morus entitled "Authoris Pro Se Defensio," it must be confessed that the general vigor with which the political arguments are pressed home is matched by the scorn with which both Salmasius and Morus are overwhelmed. It is idle to object to this or that special bit of pleading, or to urge that no decent man, much less a Christian, ought so foully to insult another. It is equally idle to claim that Milton had no right to reject the testimony as to Morus's at least partial innocence of the authorship of the "Regii Sanguinis Clamor," with its scurrilous abuse of Milton. This criticism is idle simply because it is beside the point. Milton, like every other controversialist of his time, was aiming to overwhelm his adversary. His weapon was a club, or at most a battle-axe, not the rapier Pope afterward used. He meant to fell Salmasius and Morus, and he did it by means of his superior learning, his thorough belief in the justice of his own cause, his equally thorough contempt of his adversaries, his marvellous power of writing Latin as though it were a living tongue, and finally the vibrating vigor and frequent nobility of his thought. Of their kind, then, these political broadsides, at least the first two, for it is permissible to wish that the second attack on Morus had been withheld, are masterpieces, whether the present age cares for such literary performances of vigor and scurrility or not. We need neither read them nor imitate them; but to pick flaws in them in accordance with modern notions, or to deny their greatness after their own kind, is to be distinctly unjust.

The answer to Salmasius suffers, as does so much of Milton's writing in answer to books and pamphlets, from the fact that he has to keep track of his adversary and to indulge in much antiquarian discussion. This is less the case in the "Second Defence," which is consequently much oftener quoted, though one could wish that at least the close of the answer to Salmasius, with its splendid warning to the People of England, were as well known as the hyperbolical praise of Christina of Sweden in the "Second Defence" is. Milton could have given other reasons for his praise of that sovereign besides the favor she had shown his retort to her protégé Salmasius, and he could also be proud of the fact that his noble praise of Cromwell had closed with full as noble a warning. He could likewise feel that if he indulged in a retrospective glance at his own life in reply to Morus's, or rather Du Moulin's, foul charges, he did it in a way that would make posterity his debtor, and the just pride of even Horace and Shakspere seem almost a matter of slight consequence in comparison. He could hardly with justice have looked back with such contentment on any passage in the "Pro Se Defensio," but he may be excused if he chuckled grimly over the picture he drew of Bontia's scratching the cheeks of her clerical seducer.

But perhaps it will be well to dismiss this subject of the political works — for the small tracts on the "Civil Power in Ecclesiastical Causes," on "The Likeliest Means to Remove Hirelings out of the Church," and the "Ready and Easy Way to Establish a Free Commonwealth," while interesting as throwing light on Milton's broad though not fully complete notions of toleration, his preference for an unpaid ministry, and his aristocratic hankering for a permanent Council of State, composed of the best men, are not of prime importance—by giving in outline his own defence of his habit of indulging in strenuous personalities in the course of his controversies. This defence can be found in the prefatory remarks to the "Animadversions upon the Remonstrant's Defence against Smectymnuus," and although made early in his career, will apply with full force to his later works.

The defence in question indicates, perhaps, that some mild remonstrance against his vehemence had been made to Milton by discreet friends rather than that his own conscience had been troubled in the matter. When he was defending his principles, Milton's conscience was always serene, such divine confidence did he have in his own integrity of purpose and sureness of vision. But the defence he does condescend to make of his manner of conducting a controversy is, on the whole, strong and well put, his critics being called upon to explain "why those two most rational faculties of human intellect, anger and laughter, were first seated in the breast of man," if they were not to be used against a "false prophet taken in the greatest, dearest, and most dangerous cheat, the cheat of souls." The critics might have replied, indeed, that certain faculties must be kept under by the Christian apologist or the prudent publicist, and that a debater ought not to begin by begging the question; but on the whole a majority of Milton's readers probably felt that he had defended himself well, if, in fact, many of them in that age of rough-and-ready controversy thought that he needed any defence. And we, remembering the fact that he defended none but great causes against men whom he was bound to regard as "false prophets," may surely forgive him all his errors of taste, because, in his own words, he unfeignedly loved "the souls of men, which is the dearest love and stirs up the noblest jealousy."

With regard now to the miscellaneous works we can afford to be very brief. The Logic and the Latin Grammar are of pedagogical interest merely. The state letters and papers and the small amount of private correspondence, together with the academical prolusions, are all stately, and full of historical or biographical interest, but are still minor compositions. "The History of Muscovy" is but a well-written compilation, and the "History of Britain" — most of which was probably written during his schoolmaster days — is more important, not because it has any real historical or philosophical value, but because it unfolds the early legends of British history and the chief events of the Anglo-Saxon annals with a literary power that is quite remarkable. Milton had erudition and wisdom enough to have made a great historian, at least for his times; but events determined that he should write only a picturesque and partly satiric narrative.

The tract "Of True Religion, Heresy, Schism, Toleration" is chiefly noticeable as indicating that even the Milton who in 1660 made his forlorn plea for some sort of republic was forced to accommodate himself to his times, and plead for a toleration not comprehending Roman Catholics as the only one practicable at the period, or indeed sorting with his own political principles. But the treatise "Of Christian Doctrine" is of more importance. By a curious chain of events it remained in concealment until 1823. Two years later its publication at the expense of King George IV. gave Macaulay an opportunity to write his famous essay, but produced little effect upon Anglican theology. Milton had worked upon the book for many years, developing his ideas from a most minute study of the Bible, whose ultimate authority he respected as much as he was careless of the theological opinions currently derived therefrom. Those critics are doubtless right who maintain that had the treatise been published during Milton's lifetime it would have created quite a stir. Coming to light about a century and a half later, and being almost totally devoid of eloquence and charm, it has proved of little interest save in so far as it has confirmed the impression derived from "Paradise Lost" that Milton was more or less of an Arian, and has shown that he was bold enough to oppose Sabbatarianism and to tolerate polygamy (nowhere condemned in Scripture) and the doctrine of the sleep of the soul between death and the resurrection. Had Milton's high-church and Royalist opponents but suspected him of such heresies, they might have rendered him still more obnoxious to certain not over-intelligent classes of readers, but fortune was kind to him at least in this particular, and his book is not sufficiently read now to endanger him with any one. Dr. Garnett has practically said the last word about the matter by observing that "if anything could increase our reverence for Milton, it would be that his last years should have been devoted to a labor so manifestly inspired by disinterested benevolence and hazardous love of truth."

"Disinterested benevolence and hazardous love of truth"—these are indeed the characteristic notes of Milton the man, just as strength and nobility are of Milton the writer. They emerge from any careful study of his works, but as this can be expected of but few in our fast-reading age, it is fortunate that they emerge also from many a quotable passage. Where in English, or any other literature, we may well ask, can the strength and nobility that emerge from this paragraph be matched or even approximated? —

"Then, amidst the hymns and hallelujahs of saints, some one may perhaps be heard offering at high strains in new and lofty measures, to sing and celebrate thy divine mercies and marvellous judgments in this land throughout all ages; whereby this great and warlike nation, instructed and inured to the fervent and continual practice of truth and righteousness, and casting far from her the rags of her old vices, may press on hard to that high and happy emulation to be found the soberest, wisest, and most Christian people at that day, when thou, the eternal and shortly expected King, shalt open the clouds to judge the several kingdoms of the world, and distributing national honors and rewards to religious and just commonwealths, shalt put an end to all earthly tyrannies, proclaiming thy universal and mild monarchy through heaven and earth; when they undoubtedly, that by their labors, counsels, and prayers, have been earnest for the common good of religion and their country, shall receive above the inferior orders of the blessed, the regal addition of principalities, legions, and thrones into their glorious titles, and in supereminence of beatific vision, progressing the dateless and irrevoluble circle of eternity, shall clasp inseparable hands with joy and bliss, in over measure for ever."[1]

For such prose what words of mortal praise are adequate? Organ-music the critics call it — the prose of a poet rather than strictly poetic prose — sublime, magnificent, unrivalled — all these phrases and epithets have been applied to it, and justly — but I can compare it only with something I never heard save through Milton's own mouth in "Paradise Lost," the speech of Raphael, the archangel of God.

[1] "Of Reformation in England," Book II., next to last paragraph.

CHAPTER VII

THE SONNETS

ALTHOUGH the entire sonnet-work of Milton is not equal in value to that of Shakspere, or perhaps even to that of Wordsworth, if the latter's failures be overlooked, there are reasons for maintaining that he is the most masterly of all English sonneteers. For melodious sweetness, for power to analyze and express every phase of the passion of love Shakspere, with his exquisite quatorzains, is unsurpassed; but Milton is equally so in his command of the stricter sonnet forms, in his ability to extract noble music out of them, and in his adherence to the canon that the sonnet is a short poem adapted to an occasional subject. In other words, Milton uses the sonnet more regularly and at the same time more nobly than any other English poet does, yet he has also shown his originality by imparting a special movement of his own to the stanza by omitting the pause after the eighth line that is necessary to the strict Petrarchan form. Furthermore, it is to be observed that none of Milton's sonnets is poor, that at least two-thirds are great, and that two, if not more, are grand — as grand perhaps as a short poem can ever be. It is almost needless to say that these two sonnets are the XVIIIth, "On the Late Massacre in Piedmont," and the XIXth, "On his Blindness."

Counting the Italian sonnets and the elongated sonnet *colla coda*, "On the New Forcers of Conscience," we have just twenty-four pieces, to which the Italian canzone may be added as a twenty-fifth. They were written at odd times from 1630 to 1658, the first ten (or eleven, counting the canzone), as usually printed, appearing in the edition of 1645, the remainder adorning that of 1673, save numbers XV., XVI., XVII., and XXII., which were suppressed for political reasons until 1694, when Edward Phillips gave them to the world along with the life of his uncle. Their occasional composition is plain proof that Milton used them as a means of giving a brief relief to his overcharged emotions, especially during the twenty busy years when he was cut off from elaborate poetical labors.

The first eight pieces, counting the canzone, are obviously to be classed as *juvenilia* so far as anything of Milton's can be thus classed. The first, "To the Nightingale" (1630?), is characterized mainly by charm, and hardly deserves Mr. Pattison's censure for the "conceit" that it contains. Any poet might have used the tradition about the cuckoo and the nightingale without danger of becoming a Marinist. But we must not forget to be grateful to Mr. Pattison for calling attention to the contrast Milton offers to most previous (and subsequent) sonneteers by his noble directness of phrase, his total avoidance of quip and quirk. This straightforward quality, both of expression and of feeling, is fully apparent in the second sonnet, "On His Being arrived at the Age of Twenty-three" (1631), which is as nobly autobiographical as any of the famous prose passages.

The five Italian sonnets and the canzone probably date from the continental journey and the shadowy Bolognese love affair. They are all addressed to some unknown lady save one, and that tells Diodati how much she has enslaved him. It is hard to say how sincere they are, but those of us that are romantically inclined will prefer to think that they represent a genuine, if transitory, attachment. Competent Italian critics have detected idiomatic faults in them, which was to be expected. Even an amateur can notice that in the pauses and the arrangement of rhymes in the sestet, Milton has not followed the most impeccable models, since three out of the five sonnets end in the eschewed though not prohibited couplet. But in their general spirit and matter, these sonnets are no mere exercises in a strange tongue; they are real poems by a student of Petrarch who has caught not a little of that master's subtle charm.

Sonnets VIII., XI., XII., XV., XVI., XVII., XVIII., XXIII., and the sonnet *colla coda*, group themselves as especially concerned with Milton's life under the Commonwealth. The splendid petition bidding "Captain, or Colonel, or Knight in arms" not to lift "spear against the Muses' bower," serves as a prelude to the noble encomiums on Fairfax, Cromwell,[1] and the younger Vane; the sonnet on the "Massacre of the Vaudois" is *the* trumpet note of the collection; while the second sonnet to Cyriack Skinner is the proud appeal of the defeated champion of liberty from fickle humanity to an all-seeing and all-powerful God of Righteousness. Is there a nobler passage in literature than these lines?—

> "What supports me, dost thou ask?
> The conscience, friend, to have lost them overplied
> In Liberty's defence, my noble task,
> Of which all Europe talks from side to side.
> This thought might lead me through the world's vain mask
> Content, though blind, had I no better guide."

Compared with these verses the three satirical sonnets in defence of his divorce tracts represent a much lower plane of thought and execution, but even these are fine in their way, and are proofs of Milton's astonishing mental and moral vigor.

Leaving out the grand sonnet "On His Blindness," which is too well known to require

[1] Compare the great prose tributes in the "Second Defence."

comment and is perhaps the best single illustration of the sublimity of Milton's character to be found in his works, we have in the remaining seven sonnets a series of domestic tributes to friends, two of them being elegiacal. That to a "Virtuous Young Lady," who is still unknown, is so full of charm that it ought to be quoted whenever Milton is attacked for his supposed indifference to women. Much the same thing may be said of the more highly sustained address to Lady Margaret Ley. The sonnet to Lawes on his book of Airs reminds us of "Comus," and of the fact that Milton would not let politics interfere with friendship. That to Mr. Lawrence shows us not only that Milton loved and understood young men, but that his puritanism concerned itself with the spirit of life, not with such externals as eating and drinking. The first sonnet to Skinner is perhaps fuller of moral wisdom than any other of the collection, save that on the blindness that must have fostered the wisdom.

The two elegiac sonnets are both on women, one on a hardly identified Mrs. Catherine Thompson, the other on his second wife, Catherine Woodcock. Although the sonnet form has been often used for elegiac purposes since the days of Surrey, its elaboration scarcely sorts with the partial *abandon* required of the elegy, and is better adapted to encomiastic or memorial purposes. Milton had in view both these purposes in the first sonnet, and he therefore succeeded excellently. In the second, for which he probably had, as we have seen and as Hallam long ago told us, an Italian model in a sonnet of Bernardino Rota's, affection was naturally mingled with praise; but his object was rather to impart a note of noble pathos to his poem than to abandon himself to the typical elegiac lament. Hence in this case also the elaborate sonnet form suited him admirably and he produced one of the greatest and at the same time the most affecting of his poems.

Space is wanting for any careful discussion of the sonnets from a metrical point of view, but the reader can easily get this elsewhere. It should be remarked, however, that while Milton is very careful of the rhyme arrangement of his octave, he is not over-meticulous about his sestet. Only five have the best Petrarchan sestet arrangement of three rhymes, eight run on two rhymes, regularly interlaced, and the rest are more or less irregular. This implies a free spirit which is confirmed by the innovation of allowing no pause at the end of the octave, an innovation which has practically given us a Miltonic sonnet. The carrying on of the sense and the gathered volume of sound that result, if they take away from the grace native to the verse form, add a compensating unity and dignity, and produce a true trumpet note. It is probably to the fact that his subtle ear taught Milton to make this slight change in certain of his sonnets that we owe the further fact that the sonnet on the "Massacre" is the grandest in our literature.

With the sonnets we may conveniently group, as Masson does, the miscellaneous translated poems. The rhymeless version of Horace's "Quis multa gracilis" is famous, and deservedly so. It is neither a trifle, as Masson thinks, nor "overrated," as Sir Theodore Martin opined, for it is one of the few successful examples in English of unrhymed stanzas that charm. But what shall be said of the translations of Psalms lxxx.–lxxxviii., in eights and sixes, made by Milton in 1648, or of the versions in various metres attempted in 1653? Simply, with all due respect to his memory as a consummate artist, that it is a pity he ever undertook to rival Sternhold and Hopkins, Rous, and Barton. He surpassed the framers of the "Bay Psalm Book," but he also furnished the single instance of his poetic life in which the Hebrew element of his genius was not balanced by the Greek. Of the few blank-verse translations scattered through the prose writings none seems note-worthy, although there is a touch of the true Milton in one of the versions from Geoffrey of Monmouth.

CHAPTER VIII

"PARADISE LOST"

We have already seen that Milton's masterpiece, begun in 1658, was probably completed by 1663, but not published on account of the Plague and Fire, until 1667. In view of the fact that its composition had to proceed by blocks of lines which would be retained in memory until some amanuensis or chance friendly visitor could jot them down, it cannot be said that slow progress was made, especially when it is remembered that Milton's genius seems to have been sluggish during the warmer seasons. If the presumption hold that books and maps had to be consulted by auxiliary eyes, the period of five years seems almost short; but it is not clear that even the erudition apparent in "Paradise Lost" or the traces of other authors to be discovered in it, might not have been imparted, without the intervention of books, by Milton's well-stored mind. It is indeed highly probable that much of the study that went to make the great epic was done from 1640 to 1642. There are extant four drafts of a drama upon "Paradise Lost" that date from this period, as well as a list of about a hundred subjects for epic or dramatic treatment with the theme of man's fall at their head. Thus we see that about eighteen years before he devoted himself to his masterpiece, Milton had given up the subject of King Arthur and had felt drawn to the larger topic, and we know from the splendid passage in "The Reason of Church Government" (1641) that he was engaged in study and select reading, and ordering his life chastely and nobly, that he might the better succeed in his great undertaking. There is even evidence that he had begun its composition, and that the lines in Book IV. (32-41), in which Satan apostrophizes the sun, date from about 1642. But Providence willed that the training given by study and reflection should be supplemented by that which can be obtained only from public affairs, and Milton had to become the spokesman of Liberty and England before he could be permitted to accomplish, under most grievous personal disabilities and disturbing domestic circumstances, what is seemingly the most marvellous single literary performance since "The Divine Comedy."

The English public realized more speedily than is now generally believed, what an immense boon Milton had bestowed upon it. Dryden, then high in popular favor, paid his memorable tribute, and when Addison in the next century wrote his famous critiques, he rather fanned than kindled the flame of popular interest. People already knew that Milton was sublime, that he was the most erudite of poets, that somehow out of an unfamiliar measure he had evoked harmonies hitherto unsurpassed. They knew also that if Satan was not technically the hero of the poem, he was its most interesting personage, and they doubtless saw, as we do, in his indomitable pride, a reflection of the spirit of his nobly unfortunate creator. They must have felt also, as we do, that the imaginative power that kept Milton aloft in the very heaven of heavens, that enabled him to explore the depths of hell and gave him support even in formless chaos, was something that had been absent from English poetry since the days of Shakspere. The pure charm of the scenes in Eden must likewise have seemed to them the revelation of another world of poetry than that to which they were accustomed. But are not these sensations ours? Indeed it is likely that not since "Paradise Lost" was published has there been any serious doubt about these points which are after all the only vital ones when the poem is considered as a work of art. A sublime and unique style, a powerful imagination conducting marvellous personages through the most important actions conceivable by man, a charm commensurate with the grandeur displayed,—in short, unsurpassed nobility of conception and execution,—these are features of "Paradise Lost" that no competent reader has ever failed to recognize. But our ancestors had an advantage over us in that considerations not germane to the poem as a work of art did not affect them as they do us, because Milton's theology and cosmogony were more or less theirs as well. We who have been steadily veering away from the Puritan's and even from the reformer's view of life, not only need an apparatus of theological and cosmogonical explanations, in order to understand the poem, but when we do understand it, fail in many cases to sympathize with it, fancying that we have said the last word about it when we have called it a "Puritan Epic." About this point we must be somewhat explicit.

It is quite clear, from an attentive reading of the poem, or of the criticisms that have been passed upon it, that there are weak spots in its construction which furnish persons who do not like Milton the man, with plausible grounds for attacking Milton the poet. Milton's Protestantism and his republicanism have made him obnoxious to many of his countrymen besides Dr. Johnson, and have, as a rule, limited the power and disposition of foreigners to comprehend him; hence a certain amount of harsh criticism of himself and his works has been more or less constant, and his admirers have been obliged to defend him, — a procedure which, while it has not cost him his position as a supreme classic, has certainly limited his appeal. But the most unfortunate feature of the matter is that most of the objections raised are not germane to the discussion of a work of art, and yet seem to be most important to the persons that raise them, while such as are germane ought not to bear upon the poet, since the faults stressed were inherent in the subject-matter of the poem.

For example, it is perfectly true that Adam ought to be the hero of the epic; yet it is equally true that Satan, being the more powerful personage, and having suffered more, had to absorb more of the interest, not merely of the poet, but of the reader. It is equally true that, being the real hero, — for all attempts to prove that he is not are factitious and ineffectual, — he ought not to pass out of the action so early as he does; yet this, again, was necessitated by the theme, which demanded that the expulsion of Adam and Eve should end the poem, and yet be preceded by an elaborate setting forth of the scheme of ultimate salvation for the human race. Thus Books XI.

and XII.—it will be remembered that originally the poem consisted of ten books, and that the present arrangement was effected by dividing Books VII. and X.—necessarily let the interest down almost to the lowest level at which Milton's genius could fly. Yet interest is not a primary essential of a work of art, and it may be questioned whether Milton does not deserve as much credit for extricating himself out of a difficult situation as he has received blame for a condition of things which he did not create.

Again, it is easy enough to point out the lack of humor involved in making the angels wear armor and fight with cannon; but the ability to discover the humorous quality inherent in these conceptions is purely modern. Milton could not have had it, any more than Raphael. And if we are determined to fault the incongruous in poetry, why do we not fall foul of Shakspere for making the ghost of Hamlet's father revisit the glimpses of the moon clad in complete steel? Nor could Milton have foreseen a time when men would doubt whether God would ever have allowed Satan to ruin the innocent first pair, when they would question the propriety of representing Death as the child of Satan and Sin, when they would subject the speeches of God the Father to nice metaphysical examination, based on the acquired knowledge of two additional centuries, and would demand of the angels conduct similar to that of human beings under similar circumstances. He could hardly have thought that he would ever be taken to task for making Adam wrangle with Eve, when he was only following Scripture, which he could no more have doubted or deserted than he could have doubted the existence of a personal God warring with a personal devil. He could, indeed, depart from orthodox Protestantism so far as to become a semi-Arian; but he could not desert anthropomorphism, or develop into a pantheist on the score of Copernicanism, however much he might be in sympathy with the latter. He was the child of his age, and, as Dr. Garnett well contends, is all the greater because he is representative. Finally, at least, Milton could not have foreseen that an age that had abandoned, in large part, his theology and cosmogony would ever be unjust enough not to make the same allowances for him that it makes willingly for Dante and Homer. In other words, he could never have fancied that a day would come when the critic would cease to be a judge, and would become a chameleon.

It may, then, be concluded that a majority of the defects that critics have pointed out in "Paradise Lost" are inherent in the subject or in the age and country of which the poem is representative. But they are obviously far more than counterbalanced by merits, partly belonging to the poet and his art, partly to his subject and period. Milton's style is his own, also his rare learning, which has enabled him to enrich his poem with treasures gathered from every age and clime; his own, too, is his mighty imagination, which carries him so easily to the heights of the sublime, as well as his tremendous power of invention, technically speaking, which enables him to arrange and to expand his multifarious materials. His theme and his age counted, nevertheless, for much. No mere terrestrial action could have given scope for the almost superhuman grandeur of his poem;

no age and country not Protestant could have infused into it so much mighty energy. The mediæval and Catholic Dante, as critics have pointed out, was more truly an inventor than Milton was; but he could not have invented a theme of such compelling power. In "Paradise Lost" the theme, the age, and the poet conspired as they have rarely done in the history of the world's literature; and if the result is not a universal poem like the "Iliad," — that is, a poem covering so many phases of our finite life that it seems to us universal, — it is at least the sublimest work of the imagination to be found in any language.

But here, again, fortune has been somewhat unkind to Milton. Not only has his Puritanism alienated many modern readers from him, especially extreme latter-day Anglicans, but the highest quality of his work, its sublimity, has militated against its becoming truly popular. Human nature, whatever its merits and capacities, rarely loves the heights and cannot long remain upon them. It is this failing in his readers, rather than the fact that he is the most learned of poets, and thus often difficult to comprehend, though that also counts, that chiefly limits the number of Milton's lovers to-day. It also leads otherwise competent critics to commit the blunder of maintaining that Milton is greater as a poet in youthful works like "Comus" and "Lycidas" than in his noble epic. This is like maintaining that a man in his prime is inferior, in the totality of his powers, to what he was when he was a charming youth. They simply mean in the last analysis that charm and beauty fused with budding strength attract them more than grandeur and sheer sublimity; though they would do well to observe that in the Eden portions of "Paradise Lost" charm and beauty, fused with a strength which is absolutely sure of itself, are present in full measure. Where, for example, in "Comus" or "Lycidas" shall we find a passage fuller of the true *richness* of poetry than this from the fourth book of the epic (ll. 246–256)? —

> "Thus was this place,
> A happy rural seat of various view:
> Groves whose rich trees wept odorous gums and balms;
> Others whose fruit, burnished with golden rind,
> Hung amiable — Hesperian fables true,

If true, here only — and of delicious taste.
Betwixt them lawns, or level downs, and flocks
Grazing the tender herb, were interposed,
Or palmy hillock; or the flowery lap
Of some irriguous valley spread her store,
Flowers of all hue, and without thorn the rose."

It would be, perhaps, rash to say that no such matchlessly charming effect as the close of the last verse of this passage can be found in "Comus" or "Lycidas"; but, after having edited both poems with some care, I cannot recall one.

Still it is obvious that sublimity is a rarer quality of genius than charm; or, to express it concretely, that "Lycidas" has more rivals in literature than "Paradise Lost" has. But judgment tells us that that which is rare and at the same time positively powerful deserves the highest admiration we can give, and on this verdict of judgment depend not only the hierarchies of art, but also the central truths of religion.

If now it be asked how a reader can overcome his limitations and learn to appreciate "Paradise Lost" with something like justice, a fairly satisfactory answer can at once be given. He must learn, in the first place, that a work of art should not be made the object of his religious or scientific or other preconceptions or prejudices; this is only to say that he should observe toward a poet the courtesy that the rules of good society teach him to observe in intercourse with his neighbors. He must not stand ready to do battle for his opinions on religion, politics, and the like until they are vitally assailed, which hardly ever happens in connection with a true work of art. Even in "Paradise Lost" the passages in which Milton can be justly charged with seeking positively to inculcate Puritan principles and opinions and to attack the tenets of others are few and far between; yet, if one were to judge from the way the critics talk, one would think that the great poet was forever coming down from the Aonian Mount in order to ascend the pulpit.

In the second place, the reader must, as far as possible, make his own imagination assist that of the poet, or at least, as Mark Pattison says, he must check all resistance to the artist's efforts. The resistance that the lower stages of culture always oppose to the higher must be minimized by a recourse to the aids given in abundance by commentators and editors, especially to such metrical aids as will enable us to comprehend the wonderful technique of the blank verse, without a knowledge of which half the glory of "Paradise Lost" will be forever obscured to us.

Finally, the tendency to shirk contact with the sublime must be subdued in the only possible way, by the resolute endeavor to live with the eye fixed on the heights. The best way to learn to appreciate "Paradise Lost" is to read it and re-read it. Like all great works of art, it yields its choicest pleasures only to its patient students and lovers. One might as well expect to exhaust the Mona Lisa's charm and meaning at a glance as to appreciate Milton's great epic at one reading. It is only through reading and re-reading that the full harmony of the periods will be borne upon the ear; that the majestic involution of the diction will become a help rather than a hindrance to the imagination; that the spirit will breathe freely in the courts of heaven or amid the conclaves of hell; that the pride and subtlety of the Fiend, the majestic innocence of our first parents, the single-hearted loyalty of the angels, and the ineffable purity of the Son of God will become clearly revealed to us; that, finally, the tremendous import of the drama and the marvellous and entire adequacy of the poet to its handling will hold us spell-bound yet not dazed, and make the mighty poem our possession for always, our κτῆμα εἰς ἀεί.

But, some one may say, though we may be willing to grant that foreigners have been, with few exceptions, unjust to Milton from the days of Voltaire's "Candide" to those of M. Scherer's essay, seemingly overpraised by Matthew Arnold, and though we may grant that Milton is a great poetic artist and that he made the most of his theme, we are not prepared to accept Schopenhauer's contention that interest is not a prime necessity of a work of art and we find "Paradise Lost" dull. What reply is one to make to this frank confession and avoidance? The only reply I can make is that I do not see how a powerful presentation of the story of man's fall and its attendant events can fail to be interesting to a Christian believer or even to any one who has concerned himself with man's origin and the chief explanations that have been given of it, except on the supposition, which I fear to be a true one, that men and women of certain classes are developing a growing habit of putting everything that pertains to the theory or the contemplation of religion to one side, whether it is to be taken up on one day out of seven or not at all. That such a habit exists among cultivated Anglo-Saxons, especially in this country, will not be denied, I think, by any competent observer. In spite of recent efforts to improve and increase the study of the Bible, that book is being less and less read by sophisticated people, who are, in my judgment, precisely the readers that find Milton dull. But if theology and the Bible, and talk or thought on religious subjects, are put aside for one day in the week or for good and all, it is no wonder that readers should find the theme of "Paradise Lost" dull. And if scientific views of the universe have on many minds the effect of alienating them from poetry, as they confessedly had on Darwin's, the case of Milton, who holds both by theology and by poetry, appears to be well-nigh hopeless. If he seems dull because we have relegated his subject-matter to the care of professional preachers, just as we have relegated the common and statute law to professional lawyers, or if he seems dull because his theory of the universe is childish in our eyes, then there is no way of rehabilitating him except first rehabilitating his readers.

And yet on no other suppositions than those just made can one readily or fairly account for Milton's seeming dull. Certainly for any one who accepts Christian teaching with regard to the fall and redemption of man, the superbly poetical and powerful presentation of the council of the fiends, of the war in heaven, of the bliss of our first parents and of their temptation, must possess a permanent interest unless our acceptance of these great themes be a purely conventional one. This means that at least three-fourths of the poem ought to possess permanent interest, which is a proportion that we shall find few epics exhibiting, even though we throw to the winds Poe's theories with regard to the proper length of poems. On the other hand, just as large a portion of the poem ought to prove interesting to the reader who approaches it as he does the "Iliad" with a disengaged mind. Thus, when all is said, the admirer of "Paradise Lost" is not obliged in its support to fall back upon the contention that interest is not a matter of primary concern in a work of art. It will indeed be well for any reader to develop his taste so that the rhythmical, descriptive, and structural beauties of a poem will be his first concern; but there is no reason why he should not enjoy "Paradise Lost" long before he has attained this consummation. If, however, he indulges his analytical faculties as M. Scherer and so many other critics have done, he will be certain to put it out of his power to enjoy Milton to the full. Indeed, I am simple-minded enough to fail to perceive why such analysis does not kill nearly all poetry; for it is an analysis that starts out with the assumption that a thing should be what it obviously could not have been. A certain amount of seventeenth-century Protestant theology was absolutely necessary to Milton's epic; but with the theology went along a theme of transcendent human interest and compelling power for all who accepted the theology then, or for all who are willing to realize it imaginatively now. Yet our critics, French and English, fall foul of this necessary element and rend it and then prance off proudly as a dog does with his bone. And they actually expect us to applaud them. But enough of this.

We must now pass to a brief consideration of what Milton borrowed from other poets in order to adorn "Paradise Lost." As might have been expected, he has been often charged with plagiarism, although no one since Lauder has been bold enough to forge his proofs to sustain the charge. With regard to the Bible and the classics little need be said. They are the open property of modern poets, and Milton drew from them whenever he wished. It is very difficult to tell how much he borrowed from his more immediate predecessors. According to Masson's count the number of the books that are suspected of having given him hints is so large as to be positively ridiculous.[1] The fall of man was naturally a sufficiently attractive subject to have been treated time and again in literature before he wrote. He had heard enough and read enough about it before he finally chose it as a theme, to have managed it much as he did without the aid of a single author during the period of actual composition; but it is not unlikely that, student as he was, he deliberately, at one time or another, turned over many old books or had them read to him in order that he might learn how other writers had treated the subject. From this reading he may consciously or unconsciously have received hints for his own work; but this is largely a matter of conjecture. It is likely enough, since "Paradise Lost" was first conceived as a drama, that the Scriptural play of the Italian, Giovanni Battista Andreini (1578–1652), entitled "Adamo" (1613), may, as Voltaire first suggested, have turned Milton's thoughts to

[1] Many of the works here referred to have been inaccessible to me, so that I have been forced to rely on Masson's treatment of the topic of Milton's indebtedness and on my own experience in investigating similar topics. I am inclined to be sceptical in nine out of ten cases of supposed plagiarism. I have investigated the Vondel charges.

the subject, although there seems to be not a great deal of proof that it did. Or he may have known the "Adamus Exul" of Grotius or some Latin verses by Barlæus, or any number of other now-forgotten performances. It is not at all likely that he knew anything definite of his English predecessor, the pseudo-Cædmon, first printed in 1655, when Milton was thinking chiefly about that far less savory character, Alexander Morus. It is not improbable, according to Dr. Garnett, a safe authority, that he got a hint for the idea of his diabolical conclave from the Italian reformer Bernardino Ochino. Yet after all an infernal council was a most natural starting-point for the poem, and Milton, Ochino, and Vondel might all have made Beelzebub second in command to Satan without the slightest indebtedness to one another.

The mention of the Dutch poet, Joost van den Vondel, reminds us, however, that he is the author to whom modern critics seem mostly determined to make Milton indebted. More than one book and essay have been written to prove the obligations of "Paradise Lost" to the drama "Lucifer," published in 1654, and probably more will be unless critics learn — an improbable supposition — that while tracing the literary obligations of a great poet is a harmless and interesting pursuit, it not infrequently tends to become fatuous. It is not yet proved, although it is, perhaps, probable, that Milton had Vondel's "Lucifer" read to him; it is still less clear that the verbal correspondences between the epic and the drama — most of which exist only in the shaping imaginations of the critics — are either conscious or unconscious obligations on the part of the later writer. Even the idea expressed in the famous line,

"Better to reign in hell than serve in heaven,"

may have been in Milton's mind long before he ever heard Vondel's couplet expressing the same notion. So, too, with the splendid lines in Book IV. (977–980) describing the movement of the angelic squadron which have been paralleled in "Lucifer." But granting that Milton consciously borrowed from Vondel and other poets, it would require the height of stupidity to deny that he bettered what he borrowed; and he himself has rightly contended that such appropriation is entirely admissible. The main point, however, to be remembered in this connection is that the chances are always against a poet's checking the flow of his creative impulse in order consciously and deliberately to fit into his verses an idea or image borrowed from any source whatever. If the idea or image has been assimilated by him, it may be unconsciously reproduced; but surely a want of psychological knowledge characterizes those critics who argue from every striking correspondence of thought or expression the obligation of one writer to another. In the sense that he reproduced what he had assimilated, Milton may perhaps be said to owe more to his fellows than most great poets; but in the sense that he made his verses a mosaic of other men's thoughts and expressions, he is as innocent of indebtedness as his accusers are of humor and common sense.

But we have been defending Milton long enough, and it is time to say something more positive about his masterpiece. Yet, after all, what can be said that is either new or adequate? An analysis of so well-known a poem would be out of place, an introduction to it in the shape of a discussion of its cosmogony or its theology would be equally inappropriate and useless as well, since Professor Masson has already accomplished the task in a most thorough manner. Any adequate treatment of the blank verse, which remains the allurement and despair of all poets using the English language, would be impossible within the limits of this chapter; and the same may be said of almost every single topic, such as the elaborate similes, the felicitous employment of proper names, the involution of the syntax, and the like. A discussion of the characters would be equally fruitless and unnecessary, besides holding by methods of criticism now abandoned to literary clubs, and we may therefore content ourselves with saying a few words about the rank held by the poem among the world's great epics. This is, indeed, a subject too large for full treatment here, and one on which critics are sure to disagree; but it will, at least, open up interesting fields for speculation. Before we enter upon it, however, it will be well to emphasize the fact that it is to "Paradise Lost" that the student of the art of poetry must come for his most important and inspiring lessons. If it is not the most purely artistic, elaborate work in the world's literature, it probably holds this position in English literature. All the resources of the poet's art are displayed in it in full perfection, so far as the epic form would allow. The poet's imagination may flag at times, owing to the exigencies of his subject, but his artistic power never. Hence it is a mistake to read the poem in selections, or to break off after finishing the first four books. Every page contains some marvel of rhythm or diction; nor are nine-tenths of these known to the reading public, which is in the habit of fancying that, with its short-cuts to culture, it gets at the heart of a classic author. How many people, for example, have fully realized the power of these lines from Book VII., in which Adam seeks to detain Raphael, or have gauged the *timbre* of the epithet "unapparent"?

"And the great Light of Day yet wants to run
Much of his race, though steep. Suspense in heaven
Held by thy voice, thy potent voice he hears,
And longer will delay to hear thee tell
His generation and the rising birth

> Of Nature from the unapparent Deep:
> Or, if the Star of Evening and the Moon
> Haste to thy audience, Night with her will bring
> Silence, and Sleep listening to thee will watch;
> Or we can bid his absence till thy song
> End, and dismiss thee ere the morning shine."

This may or may not be in the "grand style," but who can wonder that it induced the archangel to prolong his stay?

Turning now to the relations sustained by Milton's epic to the other great world-poems, it is a commonplace to remark that it belongs to the class of artificial rather than national or natural epics. Yet it would be unjust not to maintain that, in so far as it embodies the speculations and imaginings of Christendom on the perennially interesting and universal problems of man's creation and destiny, it partakes, through its theme, of some of the noblest and most inevitable features of those natural epics that, like the "Iliad," seem to have been born to express the greatness of a race. In other words, not only does the tremendous import of its theme add greatly to the sublimity of "Paradise Lost," it actually gives it a representative standing that is perhaps nearer to the "Iliad" than that of the "Æneid" or "The Divine Comedy." That such a claim should be made for it with regard to Dante's great poem will probably excite surprise in this day of the Italian's elevation over his English peer; but the fact remains that, although the spirit of Dante's "Comedy" represents the spirit of mediæval Catholicism, its form and substance are mainly Dante's, and, while reflecting the greatest glory upon him as an inventor, lack much of the inevitableness that attaches to portions, at least, of "Paradise Lost," to a greater degree than to any other great epic since the "Iliad."

As a work of conscious art, however, "Paradise Lost" must after all take its stand with the epics of Virgil, Dante, Tasso, and their fellows; it is *par excellence* a literary epic and cannot possess the charm of unconscious perfection to be found in Homer, or that of naïve simplicity and directness to be found in "Beowulf" and the "Nibelungenlied." But it must be observed that it does not follow that, because a poem is the result of conscious art, it is therefore inferior to a poem that springs almost naturally into existence, like a ballad or an epic founded on lays. Many readers and critics in this century suffer from what may be called "the heresy of the natural." Man has often supplemented and bettered nature in the past and he will continue to do so; on the other hand, there are occasions when he cannot touch nature without spoiling her. He can take an uninviting spot and turn it into a bower of beauty; but he lowers the sublimity of the Alps by rendering them habitable. It will not do, therefore, to make a shibboleth of the word "natural." In literature the so-called "natural" products have their own charm and power, which may or may not surpass those of consciously artistic products. For example, the "Beowulf," which is distinctly primitive and natural, would be considered equal in charm and power to "Paradise Lost" only by some philological pedant or some hopeless theorist. On the other hand, "Paradise Lost," with all its grandeur of theme and execution, could be considered equal to the "Iliad," with its natural grandeur of unconscious dignity, its divine charm, its utter inevitableness, only by a reader doomed to make Homer's acquaintance through a translation, or by one disposed to make the sublime outrank all other qualities of poetry. But "Beowulf" is as natural as the "Iliad," perhaps more so; yet while a touch of extra art would spoil the latter poem, the former might stand many such touches without loss. In the matter of syntax alone the "natural" Anglo-Saxon epic suffers greatly, not only in comparison with the modern English epic,— for Milton's involved syntax, though it has repelled many a reader, is one of the special glories of his poetic art,—but when set beside the Greek. There had either been poets before Homer, just as there had been great men before Agamemnon, or Greek syntax sprang ready armed from the former's brain; English syntax emerged more like Vulcan than like Minerva from the brain of the author of the "Beowulf." Hence consistent "naturalists" ought to prefer "Beowulf" to the "Iliad," which they probably do.

Granting now that "Paradise Lost" must perhaps rank below either of the Homeric epics, but maintaining that it surpasses even them in sublimity of imagination and all other of the natural epics in most essentials, let us endeavor to weigh it with its kindred poems of conscious art. It is obviously difficult to weigh it with works not kindred, such as Shakspere's dramas or lyrics. A great epic is certainly a rarer production than a great drama or lyric; it is rarer than a great collection of lyrics; but it is not rarer than a great body of supreme dramatic work like the Shaksperian. The plays of Shakspere taken collectively must probably rank, on account of the universal genius displayed in them, above Milton's masterpiece, though yielding to that in sublimity and perhaps in artistic perfection, technically speaking. In other words, Shakspere's genius is superior to that of Milton in range, though seemingly not in quality. But this is only to say that Shakspere alone of moderns is worthy to stand beside — no one in my judgment can stand above — the immortal singer of heroic Greece.

With regard to other dramatists and lyrists a decision is not so difficult. The collected works of none of them show universality, and Milton's genius in its power and range falls only just short of being universal. There is, therefore, no room to place any dramatist or lyrist between him and his two great superiors.

But has he not a superior in his own class of poets? If he has, it must be Dante. Tasso and Spenser may almost match him in charm, but obviously lack his power. Goethe is probably superior to him in breadth and serenity of intelligence, but falls short in sublimity, charm, and artistic power. "Faust" may appeal to us moderns on the intellectual side more than "Paradise Lost" does; but intellectual interest is a lower thing than artistic rapture. Victor Hugo on the other hand, however grandiose his conceptions and however marvellous his command of his metrical instrument, — a command in its way worthy of being compared with that of Homer or of Milton, — has not the sanity and intellectual strength and poise necessary for the poet who would successfully rival Dante or Milton. Of our great Chaucer and those often admirable narrative poets beneath him in the scale, of whom most literatures can boast a few, it is almost needless to speak in this connection. But a word must be said about Virgil. In greatness of theme, in conscious artistic mastery, in the perfection of metrical workmanship, in general intellectual balance and power, the great Roman is almost, if not quite, the equal of the great Englishman. In point of charm he seems to be superior; in point of sublimity and sheer energy he is clearly inferior. The balance will therefore tip in accordance with the relative importance allowed to charm and power in the mind of the critic.

And when all is said, this is the safest conclusion to be reached when Milton is balanced against his great predecessor, Dante. The two poets have, of course, been compared ever since the masterpiece of the later became well known; but it cannot fairly be said that their respective merits have yet been thoroughly settled. It is quite true that if a show of critical hands were made Dante would bear off the palm. He also stands better than Milton the test of cosmopolitan success. But Milton's Protestantism has been in his way in Roman Catholic countries more than Dante's Catholicism has been in his way in Protestant countries, so that the cosmopolitan test is not quite fair. There have been in this century several reactions, religious, literary, and artistic, toward mediævalism that count in Dante's favor now, but may not weigh greatly with the twentieth century. Besides, Milton has never lacked lovers like Landor, who doubted "whether the Creator ever created one altogether so great as Milton," or critics like Dr. Garnett, who, in his "History of Italian Literature," speaking of Dante as the more representative man, is nevertheless inclined to rate Milton the more highly as a poet. He has not even lacked sympathetic women admirers, like Sara Coleridge, who actually seems to have argued with Mr. Aubrey de Vere by letter as to the Italian's inferiority to the Englishman. It is needless to say that the Irish poet was not convinced, finding in Dante a charm, a humane quality, a philosophy, that he could not discover in Milton.

With regard to Dante's superiority from the point of view of charm, as well as from that of human interest, no counter plea shall be entered here. There is no passage in "Paradise Lost" so human, so touching, as the incident of Francesca da Rimini. There is probably no passage so exquisitely beautiful as that about the Siren in the "Purgatorio." In originality of conception, in the power to paint minutely vivid pictures, in his appreciation of the grandeur and sweetness of love, Dante surpasses Milton, and the latter's admirers may as well admit the fact gracefully. They may also admit Dr. Garnett's claim that Dante is the more representative man, which does not necessarily mean the greater man; and they can if they are minded admit Mr. de Vere's contention that his work is more philosophical, although wherein either poet is nowadays entitled to be considered specially philosophical might puzzle any one not a Roman Catholic or a Puritan to tell. But when Dante's admirers — and who is not his admirer? — have had their say, they must, it would seem, while rightfully asserting his strenuous dignity, admit that in sublimity, in the power to body forth tremendous conceptions, — in a word, to sound infinity, — he is Milton's inferior, and that thus very much the same balance has to be struck as in the case of Virgil. Do charm, vividness, dignity, philosophy, and the human touch outweigh the grandeur of matchless sublimity, of superhuman power, of resistless but self-controlled energy? If we answer "yes," then we must put Dante next to Homer and Shakspere; if we answer "no," then we must put Milton there. It is not a question which of the two poets we most love, which is our most constant companion; it is a question of our judgment as to which is greater; and if any man wishes to refrain from attempting such a rash judgment, who shall blame him?

Some of us are so constituted, however, that we are obliged to love and admire Milton more than we do Dante, if, indeed, we do not go the whole length with Landor and proclaim him to be the greatest of mortal men. And we have something more than the qualities of sublimity and energy on which to rest our belief in his supereminent greatness. Dante, be it spoken reverently, has faults which his admirers minimize, and Milton has merits of which his admirers have hardly made enough.

There can be little question that, with all the

advantages his human touch gives him, Dante is too personal; that his very vividness of description carries him too far. He is, at times, too local in his loves and hates to reach the proper plane of the world-poet. His very concreteness, often so great a help to him, becomes a hindrance on occasions, as when, for example, at the end of the "Inferno," he has to describe Satan. Here he becomes grotesque, just where Milton is most sublime. Then, again, Dante's "action," technically speaking, is just as liable to the charge of inconsistency as Milton's. His idealization of Beatrice is quite as much to be faulted, of course from points of view not artistic, as Milton's idealization of Satan, — a statement which merely means, in the last analysis, that critics like Mr. Aubrey de Vere have no right to grow melancholy over Milton's glorification of the principle of evil. Furthermore, Dante's age limited him, and caused him to err, every whit as much as Milton's age limited and injured him. There is a bitterness of partisanship in "The Divine Comedy" not to be paralleled in "Paradise Lost," even though we remember that Milton inserted those unnecessary lines about Limbo; there are dreary wastes of mediæval theology and philosophy in the "Purgatorio" and "Paradiso," beside which the speeches of Milton's Puritan God are luminous with interest. But Milton's faults are emphasized, while Dante's are passed over by an age reactionary enough to prefer Botticelli's mediæval types of ascetic beauty to Raphael's glorious Renaissance types of rounded loveliness.

With regard, now, to Milton's more positive merits, Dr. Garnett is seemingly right in frankly intimating that as poet, that is, as poetic artist, Milton is Dante's superior. Dante's diction and rhythm, his figures, his command of the resources of his art, are almost beyond praise; but some of us think that Milton has slightly surpassed him in every one of these particulars. The Miltonic harmonies, diction, and figures, and, one may add, general sense of proportion, are unmatched in Dante, or in Shakspere, for that matter, for the true Miltonian, and these are most important points when a balance is being struck between rival poets. But here, again, fortune has been unkind to Milton. His chief qualities, sublimity and energy, dazzle rather than attract men; and the splendors of his art produce the same effect. Dante is more human, more lovable, more endowed with what may be called the intimate features of genius. Hence he will always band his lovers together more closely than Milton will. Dante societies already exist; but there is no motion being made to concentrate interest in Milton.

But the last, and probably the most important, reason for Milton's being considered inferior to Dante by so many students of literature, is the fact that they are usually far more students than lovers of the art of poetry. Dante's great poem is fuller of symbolical and allegorical content than Milton's is, and therefore affords more satisfaction to the inquiring and probing intellect. It is also much fuller of spiritual significance of a distinctly personal kind, hence it more strongly attracts such persons as make use of poetry for moral and spiritual stimulation. These concessions will doubtless seem to many to give away Milton's case, but not so. Intellectual satisfaction and spiritual stimulation ought to be found in all great poetry — they can be obtained from a deep study of "Paradise Lost," but they are not the *raison d'être* of poetical creation, nor the main element of true poetical enjoyment. Poetry must be primarily æsthetic in its appeal, and it is clear that objective art satisfies this demand better than subjective art does. Hence it is that I rank the great objective theme of "Paradise Lost" as better poetical material than the more subjective, personal theme of "The Divine Comedy." The fact that Dante commentators are forever talking of the inner meaning of his symbolism means, in the last analysis, that elements not poetic enter largely into their enjoyment of the poem. It is the same with the Shakspere commentators, who are forever discussing psychological questions about "Hamlet." They are very shrewd and interesting gentlemen, but they seldom know much about art — if they did they would discuss "Othello" more than they do "Hamlet." Of course this is all very rash — as rash, perhaps, as it would be to tell the Browning devotees that "Childe Roland," with its delightful mystery, is not so good a poem as the simple stanzas beginning "You know we French stormed Ratisbon." People will continue to the end of time to value this poem, and that for precisely the wrong reasons, because they will persist in ignoring Greek, that is classic, standards, and in demanding mixed effects from the arts. They tell us that they get fuller results; and so they do, — results fuller of ugliness and distortion than anything that has ever come down to us from the Greeks. But we seem to be landing full in the midst of the controversy between the adherents of classic and those of Gothic art — perhaps we have been in the midst of that controversy ever since we began to discuss the merits of Milton and Dante — and we may as well extricate ourselves while we can, leaving the task of forming a Milton Society to the next generation, which may be a little less mediæval than we are.

But, after all, is there not something of moral weakness in the failure of so many Anglo-Saxons to stand up manfully for Milton's superiority to all save the two universal geniuses? It is natural for the peoples of the Continent to venerate Dante the more highly, not only because they largely sympathize with his religious philosophy, but also because sublimity of character is not one of their virtues. The Anglo-Saxon, on the other hand, though he often sinks to the depths, is of all men the most capable of rising to the heights; hence he ought to comprehend the most national of his poets. This Milton is. He is the literary embodiment of the sublime ideals that have made English liberty the dream of less fortunate peoples; he is the fullest exponent of the heroism, the steadfastness, the irresistible energy, that have planted the British outposts amid Arctic snows and the islands of the Southern seas. He is the poet of triumphant strength; his eye droops not before the Sun itself; his wings flag not in the rarest reaches of the upper ether. And yet men speaking the English tongue, and professing themselves to be proud of the achievements of their race, have had the ineffable impertinence to speak slightingly of this master spirit, and of his master work.

CHAPTER IX

"PARADISE REGAINED" AND "SAMSON AGONISTES"

THE two great poems — minor they are not in any true sense of the term — that form the subject of this chapter appeared in one volume in 1671. There is reason to think that they were printed for Milton rather than published by John Starkey on his own account. At any rate Mr. Samuel Simmons did not figure in the transaction, while the Rev. Thomas Tomkyns, the ecclesiastical censor, gave his signature to the license to print with few twinges of conscience. With regard to the dates of composition there is little available information. If Milton acted immediately upon the query of Ellwood, "But what hast thou to say of 'Paradise Found,'" it is not unlikely that the shorter epic was completed during the year 1666, or before "Paradise Lost" was published. As for

"Samson," no definite year can be assigned, but critics prefer to place it as near 1671 as they can, chiefly because its style is supposed to bear marks of old age. It is hard to say whether the harsh passages thus relied on as determining data are not the result of metrical experimentation on Milton's part, and equally hard to deny that many passages show a surprisingly youthful vigor. One may more confidently agree with the critics on psychological grounds. "Samson" is the pathetic but nobly strenuous protest of an old man against an age and country that have deserted ideals precious to him; it is the kind of protest to which Milton may have worked himself slowly up, as the last service he could do mankind. Besides, having finished two epics, the aged poet may have felt a desire to carry out his youthful purpose of writing a drama on a Scriptural subject; he had, indeed, thirty years before, considered the propriety of writing two dramas on the theme, and he may, as one may gather from his preface, have desired both to qualify the usual Puritan judgment on the drama and to censure the stage-plays then holding the London boards, as well as most of those that had hitherto been produced in England. Be this as it may, the two poems must have added to Milton's reputation and suggested by their numerous misprints the misfortune of their author.

As might have been expected, critics have differed greatly over "Paradise Regained." It is often said that Milton preferred it to "Paradise Lost," whereas he seems merely to have disliked to hear it slightingly treated in comparison with the more elaborate poem. In this he was entirely right. "Paradise Regained" is not, as Coleridge and Wordsworth thought, Milton's most perfectly executed work, but it is, as its author seems to have perceived, thoroughly *sui generis*, a masterpiece to be judged after its own kind. The reading public has not taken to it because of a preconceived notion that as a sequel to "Paradise Lost" it ought to continue the style and general interest of that great work. This, however, Milton never intended that it should do. He seized upon Christ's temptation by Satan — relying on the accounts given in Matt. iv. and Luke iv., particularly in the latter — as a parallel to the temptation of

Eve and Adam, and resolved that in Christ's triumph he would shadow forth Satan's ultimate defeat and the final acquisition of Paradise by Adam's race. He will have little or no action, but will rely in great measure upon the effects produced by the speeches put in the mouths of the protagonists. He hardly tells a story; he reports an argument in the issue of which the sequel of the first epic is found. It is evident, then, that to judge the second poem properly, one must in many respects dissociate it entirely from the first, and ask one's self whether Milton could possibly have succeeded better in the task he undertook.

It is hard to see how he could have done so, or how, with the materials at hand, he could have constructed an epic on the plan of "Paradise Lost." We need not call the sequel an epic at all unless we are inclined to agree with Masson, who follows Milton, in holding that there are two kinds of epic, one diffuse, the other brief. Neither need we look to Giles Fletcher's "Christ's Victory and Triumph," or to other poems, for Milton's model. He meant his second poem to be a spiritual exposition of a transcendent truth; he had made his former poem a sublime setting forth of an empyrean and cosmical catastrophe. As he succeeded beyond expectation in his earlier task, it is idle to talk of the later poem as his most perfect work of art, for it accomplishes its purpose no better than "Paradise Lost" fulfils its mission, and it is obviously inferior in power and scope.

But of its kind it is far more admirable than general readers seem to know. Even Dr. Garnett hardly does it justice when he asserts that it occasionally becomes jejune. From first to last its tone is that of poised nobility, which takes on at times a note of the richest eloquence known to verse. Sublimity is nowhere to be found; but poised nobility is no despicable substitute for it. Charm, too, is present, although not to the same extent as in "Paradise Lost" or in "Comus." But the peculiar note indicated is so perfect and so unique in literature, that the popular depreciation that has attended the poem seems to cast a sinister light upon Anglo-Saxon capacity to appreciate at least the subtler phases of the poetic art.

As a matter of course the mere interest of

the poem is slight. Satan, though eloquent and not yet stripped of his native dignity as "Arch-angel ruin'd," is not the wonder-compelling protagonist of the great epic. The victorious Christ is too consistently self-poised and confident of triumph to serve as a properly suffering hero, but as Dr. Garnett, whom one never tires of quoting, aptly says, "It is enough, and it is wonderful, that spotless virtue should be so entirely exempt from formality and dulness." In other words, Milton makes the most of his two characters in the situations found for him in Holy Writ. He can display his constructive invention far less than in "Paradise Lost," but, as in the latter poem, the blame must be laid on the theme not on the poet. He does display to the utmost what may be called his unfolding invention. The splendid panoramas beheld from the "specular mount" are an instance of this power perhaps unequalled in literature, and with this portion of the poem at least the world is familiar. The description of Athens is probably best known, but if it surpasses that of the Parthian array and if the latter surpasses that of the Rome of Tiberius, the difference is like that between three apparently perfect autumn days. Almost every poetical resource is brought into play, and if the rhythm is less compelling, the diction less majestic than is the case with the sublimest passages of "Paradise Lost," it is because the three themes while royally noble were not superhumanly grand. The art of the later poem may truly be said to be perfect of its kind; but it is not the supreme kind. In one respect, however, the poet's art has neither changed nor deteriorated. The wonderful use of proper names in "Paradise Lost" is completely paralleled in "Paradise Regained." Take only the passage,

"From Arachosia, from Candaor east,
And Margiana, to the Hyrcanian cliffs
Of Caucasus, and dark Iberian dales;
From Atropatia, and the neighboring plains
Of Adiabene, Media, and the South
Of Susiana to Balsara's haven."

But the typical note of poised dignity is not exemplified in these lines nor in that wonderfully beautiful passage, haunted literally by

"Knights of Logres, or of Lyones,
Launcelot, or Pelleas, or Pellenore."

Not in such truly "oraculous gems" do we find the note of the poem, but rather in the simple diction and satisfying rhythm of lines like these: —

> "Ill wast thou shrouded then,
> O patient Son of God, yet only stood'st
> Unshaken! Nor yet stayed the terror there:
> Infernal ghosts and hellish furies round
> Environed thee; some howled, some yelled, some shrieked,
> Some bent at thee their fiery darts, while thou
> Sat'st unappalled in calm and sinless peace."

Or to take a lower level and thus give ourselves the pleasure of another quotation from a work that deserved from its author the love that Jacob had for Benjamin, we find the note of poised nobility in these words of Christ: —

> "To know, and, knowing, worship God aright
> Is yet more kingly. This attracts the soul,
> Governs the inner man, the nobler part;
> That other o'er the body only reigns,
> And oft by force — which to a generous mind
> So reigning can be no sincere delight."

Turning now to "Samson Agonistes" we should notice that if it has never been a very popular poem, it has always been spoken of with the highest respect. Even Milton's Puritan contemporaries, though they might not have understood his defence of the Greek drama any more than some of his admirers have been able to understand or forgive his hypothetical change of heart with regard to Shakspere, would have been hard put to it to show how any uninspired writer could have produced a more essentially righteous and noble work of the imagination. Just so from Milton's day to our own it has been impossible, as Goethe admitted, to point to any piece of modern literature more thoroughly Greek in form and even Greek in spirit. The theme is Hebrew and the spirit, too, yet somehow the latter is also Greek in spite of the presence of Milton's characteristic diction.

It may, indeed, be contended that the theme of "Samson" hampered Milton less than the themes of any of his other great poems. It was exactly suited for dramatic treatment after the Greek fashion, and it fitted in with Milton's own temperament and experience. He, too, as every critic has pointed out, had married a wife of Philistine parentage and had suffered untold misery by her; he, too, was living blind and helpless in a state that worshipped not the true God; he, too, if he could not like Samson destroy the rulers of that people, would still cherish the hope that the English Puritans would one day rise in their might and accomplish the pious work. What wonder, then, that Milton should have turned such a theme to account in his old age, and how idle to suppose that Vondel's "Samson" influenced him appreciably.

But the peculiar dramatic form suited Milton almost as well as the theme. It required few characters, and thus his inability, which we noticed in "Comus," to create inevitable, objective personages, did him little harm. Samson was himself, or else incarnate Puritanism; the chorus did not need to be personalized; and with Manoah, Delilah, the giant Harapha of Gath, the officer, and the messenger, little play of character was required. Hence, although his weakness is perhaps apparent in a few passages, the strength and lifelikeness of his play are indisputably splendid. With a fuller action and more characters it may be questioned whether he would have succeeded so well; hence his choice of the

Greek form was not only consistent with his developed prejudice against the looser English drama, but was also a clear proof of his artistic prescience.

His artistic inventiveness was also displayed in "Samson" in marked measure, not only in his use of the incident of Harapha's discomfiture, as Dr. Garnett has pointed out, but also in the metrical construction of the admirable choruses.

He explained his metrical innovations in his preface in a *lucus a non lucendo* way by using learned Greek terms, which resolve themselves into the statement that he either avoids stanzaic divisions, or else makes his stanzas irregular, and that inside a stanza he adopts any sort of line or verse he chooses. The result of his procedure has been that it requires a carefully trained ear to appreciate the harmonies of most of the choruses. To many readers they degenerate into prose; but in view of the correctness of Milton's ear, and his unequalled command of rhythmical and metrical resources, it is unsafe for any one to pronounce any passage prosaic. The truth is, rather, that Milton has far surpassed all other English poets in producing lyrical effects without rhymes, a few of which are, however, scattered through the poem: and that, if we fail to catch the harmonies hidden in his verses, the fault is our own. Yet it may be granted, perhaps, that in some cases he has followed the Italian plan of mixing verses of various lengths, more consistently than is advisable in English, for, after all, a poem is meant to be read, and the poet must, more or less, consult the capacities of his readers.

With regard, now, to the rank of "Samson" among Milton's poems, there is little reason to agree with Macaulay in rating it below "Comus." Dr. Garnett inclines to put the two poems on a level. Pattison, after explaining how Dr. Johnson could think "Samson" a "tragedy which only ignorance would admire, and bigotry applaud," followed up his own unsympathetic treatment of "Paradise Regained" by observing that "while, for the biographer of Milton 'Samson Agonistes' is charged with a pathos which, as the expression of real suffering, no fictive tragedy can equal, it must be felt that, as a composition, the drama is languid, nerveless, occasionally halting, never brilliant." Against this uncalled-for depreciation we may well set Goethe's praise, and remark that a successful treatment of any theme in the fashion of the Greek drama could not possibly be languid and nerveless. The fact, indeed, seems to be that, in intensity of power, "Samson" is as preëminent as "Paradise Lost" is in sublimity, "Paradise Regained" in poised nobility, and "Comus" in nobility fused with charm. If this be true, Milton's latest dramatic effort should rank above his first, though it be far less popular. It might almost be held that the "Samson" is the most intensely powerful of the great English tragedies except "Lear," which is universal in its stormy passion, while "Samson" is more national and individual. If the poem shows the signs of age, as Pattison maintains, it shows them as an aging gladiator might do — the thews and muscles stand rigidly out, unclothed by youthful flesh. But the power, if naked, is all the more conspicuous and impressive.

In conclusion, let us take leave of this poem, as of its companion, "Paradise Regained," by recalling two passages typical of its spirit. The first is from a chorus:—

"O, how comely it is, and how reviving
To the spirits of just men long oppressed,
When God into the hands of their deliverer
Puts invincible might,
To quell the mighty of the earth, the oppressor,
The brute and boisterous force of violent men,
Hardy and industrious to support
Tyrannic power, but raging to pursue
The righteous, and all such as honor truth!
He all their ammunition
And feats of war defeats,
With plain heroic magnitude of mind
And celestial vigor armed;
Their armories and magazines contemns,
Renders them useless, while
With winged expedition
Swift as the lightning glance he executes
His errand on the wicked, who, surprised,
Lose their defence, distracted and amazed."

Traces of senility are hardly to be discovered in this passage, or in the following, which will serve to illustrate the staple blank verse of the drama:—

"But what more oft, in nations grown corrupt,
And by their vices brought to servitude,
Than to love bondage more than liberty —
Bondage with ease than strenuous liberty —
And to despise, or envy, or suspect,
Whom God hath of his special favor raised
As their deliverer? If he aught begin,
How frequent to desert him, and at last
To heap ingratitude on worthiest deeds!"

CHAPTER X

MILTON'S ART

It is quite obvious that a chapter with the above caption is a bold undertaking and one that is doomed from the beginning to partial or complete failure. Even a book would not exhaust the subject of Milton's art, especially in these days when it would be likely to consist in large measure of statistical tables. Then, again, there is practically nothing new to be said about a topic upon which critics great and small have exhausted themselves from the days of Patrick Hume to those of Professor Masson. Yet to close a study such as the present without an attempt to sum up the general artistic powers of the great poet with whom it has dealt, would be to leave the whole undertaking somewhat in the air; a result in which it would be cowardly to acquiesce without a struggle or at least a dignified effort.

But what now do we mean by saying that Milton was a great artist? We may mean many things, but we certainly mean that he was careful in selecting and ordering the materials out of which he composed his works, and that he was particular in joining these materials together and in preparing them for the joining process. To speak more concretely, we mean that he took great pains with his choice and evolution of theme, that he thought out the details of his composition from a logical point of view, and that in addition to this care about the thought-matter of his poems or their substance, he paid great attention to the word-matter, whether from the points of view of diction, syntax, metrical rhythm, or harmony; that is to say, to the form of his poems. This is, of course, a commonplace statement, but the two-fold division it contains will furnish us with a good point of departure.

With regard to his choice of materials, Milton, as we have observed, showed the caution that befits the scholar and the man, who, conscious of great powers, is determined to excel supereminently. He was never a hasty writer.

Up to the time of the composition of the "Epitaphium Damonis," *i.e.* his thirty-second year, he had produced what is, on the whole, a small body of verse for a poet so gifted, and had for a considerable portion of it relied upon external stimulation to production rather than upon inward prompting. In other words, if Lawes had not been Milton's friend and if King had not died, the minor poems would not now be preferred by some critics to "Paradise Lost." During the twenty years of prose writing, computing roughly, external stimulation was again the rule, as is evidenced both by the pamphlets and by the sonnets. "Paradise Lost" is the first important work representing Milton's own creative impulse, and "Samson Agonistes" is the second, for Ellwood suggested "Paradise Regained" and the theological, historical, and grammatical treatises are hardly to be considered in this connection.

As we have seen and as it has been frequently shown for the past two hundred years, Milton brought to bear on each subject, whether chosen by himself or not, the full weight of his learning and the full force of his conscience.

We have ocular proof that he was a careful reviser and that he improved what he altered; he packed whatever he wrote with erudition, sifted and fitted in to his purpose; and he studied the technic and the details of his art. He innovated and experimented, and in short prefaces explained his methods of composition. The result is that the more minute the student, the more he becomes convinced that Milton could have given a reason for every detail of his work, even for his minor variations from the normal types of his blank verse lines. This is not to say that Milton composed with meticulous care when the impulse of composition was upon him, but that the rules of his art had become a second nature to him and that his taste was as perfect as a finite man's can be. In other words, the more one studies Milton the more loath one becomes to find fault with a passage, a line, a word, — the more one comes to believe that Milton as an artist is practically flawless.

But we have already examined in some detail Milton's themes and have commented upon their evolution as well as upon the great use he made of the work of other men in carrying out his own designs. We have mentioned also, time and again, the power by which the substance of his works is fused into a poetic whole — the power of his shaping imagination. An attempt to describe Milton's imagination would be impertinent, for it would require an almost equal imagination for its successful accomplishment. It may, however, be noted that Milton's imagination seems to affect the substance of his works by limiting it to that which is noble, sublime, strenuous, or elementally pure and therefore charming. Humor is thus practically excluded as well as the intimate human note to be found in Dante and Shakspere. Pathos and sympathy exist, as, for example, in the exquisite closing passage of "Paradise Lost"; but the normal majesty of the action in each of the greater poems reduces these qualities to a minimum. In the same way, however much we may admire, with Tennyson, the paradisaic charm of the descriptions of Eden, we must admit that it is the product of an imagination that does not haunt the earth that lesser mortals tread. Milton's genius moves more freely in empyrean and cosmical spaces, and if his imagination is limited as regards certain peculiarly human spheres, it is nevertheless limitless in its own proper domain. Hence it is that in the Pandemonium scenes Milton attains to a strenuous sublimity that is probably unrivalled in literature. Hence, too, when his imagination utters itself in tropes and figures, little is definite or precise; or if precision be demanded, the spatial dimensions are large or the setting in time is indefinite, grand, unusual, or mysterious. This last point may be well illustrated by two examples taken from "Paradise Lost."

Satan is not, with Milton, the three-faced monster whose arms in length are to the height of a giant more than the latter's stature is to that of Dante; he lifts his head above the waves and

> "his other parts besides
> Prone on the flood, extended long and large,"

lie floating many a rood, as huge in bulk as Briareos or Typhon or "that sea-beast Leviathan." Here we see that the description is at first purely indefinite, and that, when a precise comparison is made, it is of such a nature that no increase of definiteness is really attained. So, too, with regard to the setting in time. The description of the splendor of Pandemonium is at first effected by means of details which are concrete only in appearance, and is then made impressive by a negative contrast with the grand architecture of far-away ancient peoples.

"Not Babylon
Nor grand Alcairo such magnificence
Equalled in all their glories, to enshrine
Belus or Serapis their gods, or seat
Their kings, when Egypt with Assyria strove
In wealth and luxury."

The latter quotation naturally leads us to consider Milton's wonderful use of proper names, and so carries us over from the substance of his poetry to its form, to its diction, syntax, and rhythm.

The ability to weave proper names into artistic verse has always been considered a good test of a poet's powers. This is due in considerable part to the fact that we realize how difficult the task is and hence rejoice as much in its successful accomplishment as we do when a poet triumphs over the intricacies of the sonnet construction. Another reason for the pleasure given us by the Miltonic employment of proper names is found in the fact that they are nearly always full of allusive charm or power and thus unlock emotions previously stored up in us. This is perhaps the prime secret of the wonderful effects produced by such a passage as that already quoted from "Paradise Regained" beginning —

"From Arachosia, from Candaor east,"

unless, indeed, the names are unknown to us and give us a sense of mysterious pleasure on the principle expressed by the adage, *omne ignotum pro magnifico*. There is another charm, too, never absent from the Miltonic roll of names — the charm of subtle harmony, and the difficulty with which this is attained enhances its power over us. It almost seems as if Milton recognized these facts from his youth, for although his ability to use proper names culminated in his mature poems, it is found in his earliest experiments. At least it is evident that it brought his erudition most happily into play, and that it is one of the most characteristic features of his style.

With regard now to his diction in general there is nothing to say that is not already familiar. His total vocabulary is but little over half that of Shakspere; but this does not mean much when we remember that Milton was the more careful artist and that whole ranges of Shakspere's work, such as the scenes of low comedy, were outside of the later poet's purview. Besides, Shakspere wrote in a period famous for the flexibility of its vocabulary, and the number of words employed by him that have lost currency seems to be greater by a considerable amount than the number of similar words in the case of Milton as a poet. It is more important to observe that if Milton's poetic diction does not, like Shakspere's, suggest the idea of lavish affluence, it never suggests poverty, but rather just proportion. The chances are that Milton's knowledge of words was as large as Shakspere's, but that the nature of his subjects and the purity of his taste limited his use to what is nevertheless a very considerable number. Of the words he does employ quite a large proportion will naturally be found to be of Romance or Latin rather than of Anglo-Saxon origin. With his themes it could not well have been otherwise; besides the longer Latinistic words conduced to the desiderated sonorousness of his verse. Yet, as Masson has well shown, the Saxon words are those most frequently used, amounting in some passages to ninety per cent and rarely falling below seventy. Hence his poetry, for all his erudition, is English in its warp and woof.

With regard to his syntax, the case is somewhat different. The influence of the masses of Latin that he read and wrote is plainly perceptible in the closely knit, involved, and often periodic and lengthy sentences in which his mature works abound. This is not true of many of the earlier poems, such as "L'Allegro," which have a looseness and directness of syntactical arrangement that are both English and Elizabethan. Even in "Comus" and "Lycidas," which are by no means wanting in Latinisms, there are few passages that exhibit the involution characteristic of "Paradise Lost." This involution is, indeed, practically unmatched in our poetry. It finds little place in the work of Shakspere, who, while capable of every sort of style, and full of syntactical resources, is in the main straightforward, not to say loose, in the construction of his sentences. This very looseness, culminating, as it often does, in an impetuous piling up of ideas or images, frequently renders Shakspere difficult reading, especially to young persons; but his most tangled passages seldom strain the attention and the powers of comprehension of his readers as fairly normal passages of "Paradise Lost" strain Milton's would-be admirers.

There can be little doubt that this fact accounts for much of Milton's comparative unpopularity. But is his syntax at fault? It surely is, if we may apply strictly Mr. Herbert Spencer's principle, that it is necessary to economize the reader's powers of attention. Yet this principle cannot apply to poetry, if it can be shown that the poet's style, while straining the average reader's attention, really assists the capable imagination. And Milton's involved diction does this. His unique themes require a unique style. If he had dealt with human beings, as Shakspere did, he would doubtless have used a more straightforward style; but he needed to get his readers away from

> "the smoke and stir of this dim spot
> Which men call Earth,"

and therefore he required a style not natural or familiar to them. Their mental energies once engaged, he could count the more surely upon stimulating their imaginations, and could then lift them up on the wings of his supreme genius into the heaven of heavens. Long, involved, periodic sentences also helped him to obtain sonorousness, and, as we shall soon see, were essential to the full success of his blank verse. Besides, his Latinistic syntax removed his style still further from that of prose, thus making it essentially poetic, and better capable of bearing the weight imposed upon it by the sublime structure he was intent upon rearing. That Milton, in particular passages, pushed the principle of involution too far, has, indeed, been admitted by his greatest admirers; but against such admissions we must always set his own almost flawless taste. The "grand style" Mr. Arnold was so fond of praising, would not have wholly disappeared from "Paradise Lost" had that poem been written in a straightforward, uninvolved manner, but its occurrence would have been much rarer; it certainly would not have been found on every page.

But an example will prove more than several pages of critical exposition. Let the reader imagine the following passage, or any similar one, stripped of its involution, and divided up into comparatively short, straightforward sentences!

> "Not that fair field
> Of Enna, where Proserpin gathering flowers,
> Herself a fairer flower, by gloomy Dis
> Was gathered — which cost Ceres all that pain
> To seek her through the world — nor that sweet grove
> Of Daphne, by Orontes and the inspired
> Castalian spring, might with this Paradise
> Of Eden strive; nor that Nyseian isle
> Girt with the river Triton, where old Cham,
> Whom Gentiles Ammon call and Libyan Jove,
> Hid Amalthea, and her florid Son,
> Young Bacchus, from his stepdame Rhea's eye;
> Nor, where Abassin kings their issue guard,

Mount Amara (though this by some supposed
True Paradise) under the Ethiop line
By Nilus' head, enclosed with shining rock,
A whole day's journey high, but wide remote
From this Assyrian garden, where the Fiend
Saw undelighted all delight, all kind
Of living creatures new to sight and strange."

It will be observed that this sentence, while lengthy and marked by involution and strict syntax, is periodic only in its first section. The addition of the two other sections, each beginning with "nor," makes it, in the technical sense, "loose," and this is the case with many of the longer sentences. But Milton, who was as careful of his punctuation as of his spelling, must have had some reason for making such sentences trail, and it may be presumed that this reason is to be found in a metrical consideration. He did not wish the reader to pause any longer than was necessary for the purpose of breathing, but to go straight on and thus allow the passage to produce the effects of metrical unity. For as Wordsworth perceived long ago, the Miltonic blank verse does not move by lines but by passages of varying lengths. In the manipulation of such passages Milton is unique and supreme. They are long, short, and of medium length, and are infinitely varied in their succession; and in their management, if anywhere, the secret of Milton's organ music is to be found. Not that individual lines and small groups of lines are not harmonious and sonorous — for they plainly are. But the rhythmic and harmonic effects of these parts of the whole rhythmic period blend into the grander rhythmic and harmonic effect of the period itself, and our reading is faulty if it does not bring out this fuller and final effect. When we compare Milton's blank verse with that of most other English poets except Shakspere, we find either that the period hardly exists for us or that it exists on a much less varied and noble scale. For example, in Thomson the periods constantly include but three or four verses, and end at the close of a verse with a uniformity that Milton avoids.

But we are now fairly upon one of the most fascinating and intricate problems connected with Milton's art, and the limits of our space warn us that we must be careful as to the questions we open up. Quite an essay might be written upon Milton's rhythmical periods whether in "Paradise Lost" or in "Lycidas." So, too, much may be said about his use of rhyme in his youthful poems as well as about his experiments with stanzas and with unstanzaic rhymeless lyrics — points that have been already dealt with briefly elsewhere. But here only a few somewhat desultory remarks will be possible.

Readers of Milton's blank verse, just as readers of Chaucer's couplets, must beware of thinking that either poet counted his syllables or used a metronome. Milton's normal blank verse line consists, it is true, of ten syllables, accented alternately from the second; but he sometimes admits a redundant eleventh syllable in his epics and frequently does it in "Comus" and "Samson" where the verse naturally takes on the freedom allowed it in the drama. He also permits himself redundant syllables in the body of a verse, because his ear was satisfied if it got a sufficient number of stresses in a line — normally five — to make it fairly uniform with its fellows and at the same time secure the charm of play and variety. The verses that make modern readers halt are generally those in which an accent has been shifted since Milton's day, or in which a tendency to count syllables rather than be satisfied with an approximate rhythm, has baffled the inexpert reader.

For example, the verse:

> "And sat as Princes whom the supreme King"

seems prosaic until we learn that Milton intended "supreme" to be stressed on the penult. The verse describing Leviathan, which God

> "Created hugest that swim the ocean stream,"

confuses us until we learn that Milton meant us to read straight along just as if we were reading prose, in which case we should pass rapidly over the two offending syllables in the third foot.

Finally, for in this matter we must be brief since Professor Masson and Mr. Bridges have dealt with it at length, the line

> "That invincible Samson, far renowned,"

ought, it would seem, to be read with equal straightforwardness, when it will be at once perceived that although only four stresses are thus obtained, the verse will fit sufficiently well into its period. We shall probably not attempt, if we are wise, to stress "that," and we shall do well to remember that after all in the reading of blank verse, as well as of prose, not a little depends upon the idiosyncrasies of the reader.

But perhaps the most important point to be observed about Milton's blank verse is his management of the cæsura or pause in the individual line. It is in this particular that he best earns the title of supreme metrical artist of the world. Infinite variety and infinite resulting harmony characterize his manipulation of these pauses, which may fall almost anywhere within the limits of a line. The reader should train himself to observe their effects, and should follow his common sense in finding them. If he read intelligently he will be almost sure to pause where Milton wished him to, and if he have an ear capable of appreciating harmony he will often be tempted to pause longer than is proper, in order that he may admire such splendid rhythmical effects as this: —

"The Ionian Gods — of Javan's issue held
Gods|, yet confessed later than Heaven and Earth."

With regard, now, to the lyrical verse in general, it must be owned that, although in "L'Allegro," "Il Penseroso," parts of "Comus," and one or two other early poems, Milton caught the melody and the swing of the Elizabethan octosyllabics, he was not a true singer of songs, but more a lyrist of the elaborate kind. His work is rather harmonious than melodious; it is constructed, but does not flow. Great success has, of course, been had in the elaborate lyric, — which for Anglo-Saxons culminates, perhaps, in "Lycidas," "Alexander's Feast," and the "Ode on the Intimations of Immortality," — but it is obviously less true than the simple lyrics, of which one of Shakspere's or Burns's songs may be taken as typical, to the essential function of lyric poetry, which is the singing out of the heart of the poet. Milton was not made to sing out his heart; hence, while he can give us the beautiful "Echo Song" in "Comus," his highest and most characteristic work is to be found elsewhere. Yet one hesitates in pronouncing this judgment, for where in English literature can a more exquisite passage of lyrical poetry be found, one combining more of the charm of well-chosen rhymes and melodiously flowing verses, than at the close of "Comus"?

Side by side with Milton's inability to sing out his own heart must be set his comparative inability to body forth, in dramatic form, the thoughts and feelings of others. We have already referred to this limitation of his genius in connection with "Comus" and "Samson." Curiously enough, although he is not a simple lyrist, and thus is not able to sing a perfect song, it is to his possession of certain of the characteristics of a true lyrist that his failure as a dramatic poet is due. Milton himself, or some phase of his character, speaks through all his personages, but when one's personality speaks, one is, to a certain extent, a lyrist. Hence it is that Milton belongs to that class of quasi-dramatists of whom Mr. Theodore Watts-Dunton treats, in his admirable article on "Poetry" in the "Encyclopædia Britannica." He was greater than the simple lyrists in that he could not help concerning himself with the fortunes of others, but he was still enough of a lyrist always to be mindful, consciously or unconsciously, of himself whenever he attempted dramatic work. In other words, he could not, any more than Dante, attain the objectiveness of Homer, Shakspere, and Chaucer at his best. But at times he came near doing this, perhaps most conspicuously in the speeches of Satan and Christ in "Paradise Regained," and there is always such tremendous power in his conception and representation of his characters, that his failure on the score of objectivity of treatment is almost overlooked. Indeed, it is not quite certain whether the power of representing characters objectively, *i.e.* dramatically, is *per se* greater than the power of representing them epically, with an infusion of lyrical passion. The main test in such cases must be the rarity of the power, and, on the whole, the thoroughly great quasi-dramatists are not more numerous than the thoroughly great dramatists.

Nor is it absolutely clear that the universality of range and power that we commonly attribute to Homer and Shakspere alone is, from the point of view of art, superior to stupendous power realizing itself in sublime and noble creations. After all the universality is more apparent than real; and the limitations observable in connection with supreme power of the Miltonic order, are often self-limitations. In other words, it is as true to say that Milton would not have written many of Shakspere's scenes as that he could not have written them. In the preceding pages deference has been paid to current critical opinion by placing Milton below the universal poets; but sometimes this seems to be an injustice to him, since, in Landor's words, it is doubtful whether God "ever created one altogether so great as Milton." Be this as it may, we should remember that in limiting his universality, reference is made chiefly to the range of his work from the point of view of its contents, not from the point of view of its style or form. Neither Homer nor Shakspere is universal from the latter point of view. Homer is epic and dramatic in a supereminent way, but he is not thus great as a lyrist. Shakspere is supreme as a dramatist and lyrist, but his narrative poetry, beautiful as it is, does not place him among the truly great writers of epic.

Closely connected with this matter of Milton's lack of universality is a quality of his work that demands special mention — his virility. While it is a slander to represent Milton as incapable of appreciating woman, it is quite true to say that she plays no exalted part in his work — for Eve before her fall is practically extra-human — and that the poet himself is above all characterized by virility. The treatment of women in the youthful poems and in some of the sonnets, prevents us from saying broadly that Milton could not successfully introduce the sex into his poetry; but it is obvious that one of the specially charming features of the Shakspe-rian and Homeric creations is wanting to his work. Here, again, fortune has been unkind to Milton, for the world, ever since his day, has been paying more and more honor to women, until it almost looks as if they had ousted, or would soon oust, man from his position as the main subject-matter of literature. As a result women, who seem to be the chief readers to-day, do not as a rule care for Milton — sublimity of character not being one of their virtues any more than it is of the continental nations. Hence it is almost idle to hope that Milton can ever become truly popular until women are educated up to the conception and realization of sublimity, as they surely will be. Meanwhile it will be perhaps not impertinent to ask whether, from the point of view of art, Milton's superhuman personages may not be put in the scales with Shakspere's men and women and balance them. The one set of characters is as unique as the other, and it is mainly personal preference that makes it so easy for the average reader to decide between them.

But it is time to draw this chapter and this book to a conclusion, and this may be not inappropriately done by proposing and attempting to answer a query with regard to the two supreme poets whom it is England's imperishable glory to have given to the world. The query is — Can an unmistakably Shaksperian passage in the "grand style" be set beside an equally unmistakable Miltonic passage in the "grand style" and the distinguishing notes be concretely and adequately registered? If they can be, the reader will have one of those touchstones Matthew Arnold was fond of using, or rather one of those tuning-forks, that will enable him to contrast the two poets when at the highest reaches of their art and to determine when each falls short of his supreme work. Such a practical test thoroughly applied will conduce to more adequate knowledge and more perfect love of the two master-poets than the mere perusal of any number of critical lucubrations. It is, of course, idle to hope that any such unfailing test can be given in these pages, but one can perhaps be adumbrated.

Let us take two Shaksperian passages and two Miltonic ones.

The Prologue to "Troilus and Cressida" opens thus: —

"In Troy, there lies the scene. From isles of Greece
The princes orgulous, their high blood chafed,
Have to the port of Athens sent their ships,
Fraught with the ministers and instruments
Of cruel war."

Othello's last speech of consequence runs in the main thus: —

"I pray you, in your letters,
When you shall these unlucky deeds relate,

Speak of me as I am; nothing extenuate,
Nor set down aught in malice: then must you speak
Of one that loved not wisely but too well;
Of one not easily jealous, but being wrought
Perplex'd in the extreme; of one whose hand,
Like the base Indian, threw a pearl away
Richer than all his tribe; of one whose subdued eyes,
Albeit unused to the melting mood,
Drop tears as fast as the Arabian trees
Their medicinal gum. Set you down this;
And say besides, that in Aleppo once,
Where a malignant and a turban'd Turk
Beat a Venetian and traduced the state,
I took by the throat the circumcised dog,
And smote him, thus."

Against these unmistakably Shaksperian passages let us set these from "Paradise Lost."

"And now his heart
Distends with pride, and, hardening in his strength,
Glories: for never, since created Man,
Met such embodied force as, named with these,
Could merit more than that small infantry
Warred on by cranes — though all the giant brood
Of Phlegra with the heroic race were joined
That fought at Thebes and Ilium, on each side
Mixed with auxiliar gods; and what resounds
In fable or romance of Uther's son,

> Begirt with British and Armoric Knights;
> And all who since, baptized or infidel,
> Jousted in Aspramont, or Montalban,
> Damasco, or Marocco, or Trebisond,
> Or whom Biserta sent from Afric shore
> Where Charlemain with all his peerage fell
> By Fontarabbia."

And again: —

> "Yet not the more
> Cease I to wander where the Muses haunt
> Clear spring, or shady grove, or sunny hill,
> Smit with the love of sacred song; but chief
> Thee, Sion, and the flowery brooks beneath,
> That wash thy hallowed feet, and warbling flow,
> Nightly I visit: nor sometimes forget
> Those other two equalled with me in fate,
> So were I equalled with them in renown,
> Blind Thamyris and blind Mæonides,
> And Tiresias and Phineus, prophets old:
> Then feed on thoughts that voluntary move
> Harmonious numbers; as the wakeful bird
> Sings darkling, and, in shadiest covert hid,
> Tunes her nocturnal note. Thus with the year
> Seasons return; but not to me returns
> Day, or the sweet approach of even or morn,
> Or sight of vernal bloom, or summer's rose,
> Or flocks, or herds, or human face divine;
> But cloud instead and ever-during dark

Surrounds me, from the cheerful ways of men
Cut off, and, for the book of knowledge fair,
Presented with a universal blank
Of Nature's works, to me expunged and rased,
And wisdom at one entrance quite shut out."

Now what is one to say of these contrasted passages, or rather, what is one not to say of them? How perfectly supreme each is, and yet how different! And how many artistic qualities may be pointed out in each! Is it not idle, then, to attempt to differentiate them? Probably it is; yet are not superb and glorious affluence, and gathered-up human strength, and piercing human sympathy the distinguishing notes of these, and most other great Shaksperian passages; while sublime nobility and godlike poise of reticent power are the distinguishing notes of these and most other great Miltonic passages? Does not Shakspere always address us in the infinitely varied voice of the ideal and perfect man, and Milton in "that large utterance of the early gods"? It is the noontide Renaissance set over against an age that never existed, an age characterized by a blending of the best characteristics of the Greek and the Hebrew. Shakspere is the full blushing rose of human genius in its totality; Milton is the stately, pure, noble lily of human genius on its spiritual and ideal side. Let us give our best love to the one or the other; but let us reverence both with all our hearts and souls.

INDEX

N.

O.

P.

www.ingramcontent.com/pod-product-compliance
Lightning Source LLC
Chambersburg PA
CBHW020943120726
47905CB00008B/2653